BRIDGE ACROSS THE AMERICAS

FAVORITE HISPANIC STORIES

PENNY CAMERON

Language & Culture Center
University of Houston

Dominie Press, Inc.

ACKNOWLEDGMENTS

The author would like to thank the following people for their help and advice:

Leonardo Calado de Brito — Brazil
Lic. Edmundo Juan Daniel de Hoyos Lozano — Houston, Texas
Gustavo Franco — Zacapa, Guatemala
Dr. Lane Roy Gauthier — University of Houston
Oscar Ranato Hernandez — Houston, Texas
Judy Kleeman — Houston Community College
Donna Kruszewska — Houston Community College
Carl R. Lindahl — University of Houston
Jeanne McDonough — University of Houston
Maryann O'Brien — University of Houston
Bobbie Peters — Houston Community College
Dorothy Sampson — Houston Community College
Devi Spencer — University of Houston
Christine Tierney — Houston Community College
Carlos A. Vesga — Houston, Texas
Lammoglia Villagomez — Houston, Texas
Louise A. Wooten — Houston Community College
Dr. David J. Yaden — University of Houston

Publisher: Raymond Yuen
Executive Editor: Carlos Byfield
Editor: Karen Hannabarger
Cover Illustrator and Designer: Jennifer Hewitson
Text Illustrator: Diana Bennett

 Dominie Press, Inc.
5945 Pacific Center Blvd., Suite 505
San Diego, California 92121-4309

ISBN 1-56270-017-0
Printed in U.S.A.

2 3 4 5 6 7 8 9 AG 98 97 96 95 94 93 92

CONTENTS

INTRODUCTION TO THE TEACHER

RATIONALE

ecent reading research suggests that students will learn to read more easily if we activate their schemata before they start to work on a text. (A schema is the knowledge of the world that a person has accumulated in a life time. Schemata is the plural form.) Such activation of their schemata will let the students bring what they know to the text and interact with it.

It follows that the illustrations should give the reader a preview of the story, and there should be pre-reading questions and activities to appropriately direct the reader's attention. Students can then employ top-down reading strategies, working from whole to part, and making intelligent guesses at individual lexical terms. For example, students who know the story of La Llorona know that she suffers from terrible grief and remorse. They are likely to be able to deduce the meaning of weeping, even if they have not encountered the word before. They can also employ bottom-up strategies; for example, they will reason that discontent is the negative form of content. Then they are working from part to whole, another valid way to seek meaning.

The rationale behind these stories and exercises, written primarily but not exclusively for people who have ties to Latin America, follows:

- People learn to read by using what they know. These stories have been chosen for their familiarity, so the students will feel at home.

- Students must be actively involved in the reading task. At the beginning of each story students will be challenged to deduce the meanings of some vocabulary items by completing a task, e.g., a crossword or a matching exercise. This is pre-teaching in disguise, and is intended to make the students participate in learning the meaning of the new words. It is best done as a cooperative learning exercise and should be checked before the story is read.

- Traditional stories are suitable for both children and adults. We can have a high degree of confidence that traditional stories will be familiar to the largest possible segment of Latin American students.

- Traditional stories have simple story grammars. The narrative structure has been refined over the years, and the expository structures are clear.

For example, a traditional story will not indulge in flash-backs; the narrative proceeds in chronological order.

- The exercises are designed to let students employ top-down and bottom-up strategies. They are varied so the student will have to think, not simply learn how to do the same exercise over and over. The questions and exercises will include discussion of the illustrations to activate the students' schemata. There are oral and written questions to involve the students in the story and comprehension and vocabulary questions, but they will not always take the same form. There are word-recognition exercises and games and follow-up exercises where appropriate.

- Some of the students who read these stories will come from cultures where a particular traditional story does not exist or exists in a different form. The questions about the illustrations are designed to prevent the student from engaging the wrong schema.

- Internal glosses of key words help the reader. Wherever possible, a new word will be explained within the text. (e.g., "He knows he's blushing, because his face is red and hot.")

- Students are encouraged to re-read the text when answering questions. They should use the context and not regard the exercises as memory tests.

- The stories are short, to give a sense of fulfillment — a quick reward.

- The syntax is controlled. Sentences are short, and figurative language is avoided. Passives and subjunctives are avoided wherever possible, although *wish*, *want*, and *think* are used.

- The stories are graduated in difficulty; those at the beginning of the book are easier that those at the end.

It is impossible to separate vocabulary from comprehension at high beginner/low intermediate levels. The pre-reading activities introduce new vocabulary, the post-reading questions enlarge upon it, and the discussion and invention questions provide an opportunity for using the new words. Comprehension questions and exercises usually involve group work. These questions range from those that can be answered directly from the text to those that draw upon the students' own experiences. Because the students still have limited language to express themselves, discussion and invention questions are simple and relevant to the story and/or the students' lives.

STRATEGIES IN THE CLASSROOM

ou can do what a book cannot — perceive the strengths and needs of the student. The pre-reading questions are intended to activate the readers' schemata, to make them apply what they know to the text. The "Using What You Know" exercises are designed to provide some of the vocabulary your students will need.

No teacher should feel limited by what is in a text. If you think of questions or activities which will trigger something in the minds of your students, use them. You know your class better than anyone else.

If at all possible, read the story aloud to your class and have them read along with you silently. Students learn a great deal about suprasegmental features such as pitch, pace, emphasis, and rhythm by listening to the teacher read. Reading aloud helps the students to understand the story and to avoid miscues.

It's helpful if students read the story at least twice before they try to answer the questions. Read the story aloud while the students follow and mark unfamiliar words. Immediately read the story again, and ask the students to flag words that are still unfamiliar after the second reading. The number of unknown words is usually reduced by 50 percent simply by reading twice, and this is not lost on the students. Alternatively, the students may read the story silently in class before you read to them, or they may read it as a homework assignment and read it aloud themselves in class. Students may be asked to identify their favorite part of the story and to read it aloud.

Some students resist the idea of reading to the end of a sentence to get clues to unknown words. The following exercise may help.

Write on the board:

Let's go _____ (fishing, shopping, flying, swimming).

Tell the students they must choose one word.
Then write:

Let's go _____ (fishing, shopping, flying, swimming) in the mall.

Ask the students which word is right in the second sentence. Ask them how they know.

You may want to repeat the exercise with other sentences, for example:

I like to _____ (eat, drive, run, finish).
I like to _____ (eat, drive, run, finish) my car.
I want a _____ (tiger, tree, fan, mountain).
I want a _____ (tiger, tree, fan, mountain) to put in my garden.

ESL students are often very slow to respond to a question. Wilson and Cleland suggest waiting three to five seconds, thus allowing students time to think and form their responses and to elaborate them.

When an exercise calls for a pictorial response, encourage the students to draw quickly. Stick figures are ideal. The value of the exercise lies in the explanation of the drawing to other students. Pictorial responses may be done as small group or blackboard exercises.

THE STORIES THEMSELVES

 ome of these stories belong to a particular place, and where this is the case it is mentioned in the script. La Llorona's tragedy plays itself out in Mexico City, but there are many other versions of the same tale, usually involving a woman who has been seduced and then deserted by a conqueror. The tale of the shark hunter is told in many cities by the sea: the version in this book is from Puerto Rico, but a student told me he knew the story as part of his lore of his home town, Santa Cruz, in Mexico. Juan Diego belongs forever to Mexico, and tricksters like Pedro de Urdemalas belong everywhere from Chile northward. A student from Argentina knew Pedro under another name, and his exploits were familiar to the Ecuadoreans. The same applies to the unfortunate Bobo: stories about fools abound, and cross national boundaries as if they were not there.

Indeed, where traditional stories are concerned, national boundaries might not exist. The same stories come to light again and again, perhaps made local by a particular twist, but familiar in outline, and that is a large part of their charm. We must thank the traveling tale tellers who passed them on to us, honing and refining them at every telling, century after century. ▲

PEDRO DE URDEMALAS AND THE PIGS' TAILS

BEFORE YOU READ

Answer the following questions.

1. Can you identify a pig's ears, feet, and tail?
2. What do you see in the illustration?

USING WHAT YOU KNOW

Find the meaning for each word. Then write the letters of the correct meanings on the line. One has been done for you.

__d__	1. kind	a.	large farm
_____	2. ranch	b.	soft, wet land
_____	3. pigpen	c.	someone who does not tell the truth
_____	4. swamp	d.	good
_____	5. weep	e.	place to keep pigs
_____	6. liar	f.	cry very sadly

edro de Urdemalas was a liar who loved to trick people. He did not tell the truth.

One day, Pedro was feeling very sorry for himself. "Oh, my poor head," he moaned. "It hurts so much. What did I do last night? Why did I stay out with my friends? Why did I drink so much?"

He opened his eyes a little bit. The sun looked very bright. He shut his eyes again. He felt very sick.

Pedro walked along a road until he came to a ranch. The farmer raised pigs. Pedro stood for a long time and looked at the pigs in their pigpens. He looked closely at their tails.

"They're so different," he thought. "Some pigs' tails are short and curly, and some are long and straight. Other tails are very fat. And everywhere there is a pig, there is a pig's tail."

He could feel an idea coming into his mind. He thought some more. "Everywhere there is a pig, there is a pig's tail. And everywhere there is a pig's tail, there is a pig."

The idea grew bigger and stronger. Then Pedro had a plan. He took out his old knife. He climbed over the fence into the pigpen. Pedro caught the first pig. He cut off its tail. Then he cut the tails off all the other pigs.

Pedro walked on. Soon he came to a swamp. He put his hand into the mud of the swamp. It was very soft.

Pedro buried the pigs' tails in the swamp. Only the ends stuck out. Then, he sat down under a tree.

Pedro rested until he saw a man on a horse. The man was coming toward him. As soon as the man came close, Pedro began to weep.

"What is the matter?" the man asked. He had a kind face.

Pedro pointed to the swamp. The pigs' tails were sticking up in the air. "All my pigs have died in this swamp," he moaned. "I have lost everything. I have no money, no future, no hope."

"Please don't cry," the kind stranger said. "I'll buy your pigs from you. Then I'll send my servants to dig them out of the swamp. How much do you want for them?"

"I loved my pigs," Pedro sniffed. "But I can see that you are a good man. You have treated me with great kindness. I will sell the pigs to you for one thousand dollars."

The stranger gave Pedro one thousand dollars. Pedro pretended to weep some more. As soon as the stranger left to get his servants, Pedro jumped up and ran away.

Pedro wandered on. He lived well until the one thousand dollars was gone. But the day came when he needed money. Pedro needed another plan to trick an innocent person. And that's another story. ▲

UNDERSTANDING WHAT YOU READ

A. *Tell if these sentences are true or false. Write* true *or* false *on the lines.*

true   1. Pedro was a liar.

_____ 2. Pedro was feeling sick.

_____ 3. Pedro became a better man at the end of the story.

_____ 4. Pedro owned the pigs.

_____ 5. The stranger was kind.

_____ 6. The stranger was clever.

_____ 7. The stranger's servants dug up the pigs.

B. *Circle the words that best complete the sentences.*

Pedro de Urdamalas was a (good, bad, truthful) man. He (walked, drank, cut off) some pigs' tails and buried them in a (swamp, farm, pigpen). A (kind, old, sick) stranger bought the pigs' tails. The stranger thought he was buying (pigs, a swamp, trees). Pedro (stayed to talk, ran away, went home).

VOCABULARY

A. Use the following words to fill in the blanks.

weep   ranch   liar   swamp

1. My friends are farmers. They have a big _____ where they raise pigs.

2. You are a _____. You say you came home, but I know you did not.

3. There was so much rain that the lawn was like a _____.

4. I'm so unhappy, I just want to _____.

B. Write your own sentences using the words below.

weep   _____

_____

liar   _____

_____

ranch   _____

_____

swamp   _____

_____

DISCUSSION

1. How do you think the kind man felt when he found out he was fooled?
2. What sort of man was the stranger?
3. How do you feel about liars?
4. Do you think this story is funny? Why? Why not?
5. Do you know any other stories about tricksters?

LA LLORONA

BEFORE YOU READ

Answer the following questions.

1. Do you know the story of La Llorona?
2. Have you heard the wind blowing? Does it sometimes sound like a woman crying? What do you think?
3. Do you know what a ghost or a phantom is?
4. What do you see in the illustration?

USING WHAT YOU KNOW

Look at the following words. Five of the words are about being sad. Four of the words are about being afraid. Circle the words that are about being sad.

sob	frightened	crying	scared	weeping
cry	terrified	afraid	wailing	

his is the story of La Llorona. It all happened more than four hundred years ago, in the middle of the sixteenth century.

Once there was a woman with a cruel heart. She was called La Llorona. She liked to hurt people. She was so mean that she killed her own babies.

La Llorona took her new little baby son to the canal outside Mexico City. She held him under water until he drowned. Then she went away.

La Llorona killed several babies like this. After a while, she began to feel very sad. She knew that she had been very wicked. She walked through the city at night, weeping and crying. She was looking for her children.

One night a soldier was standing at a gate. It was his job to stop people from going in. The soldier was very sleepy. In fact, he was more than half asleep. La Llorona came to him and said, "What time is it, soldier?"

The soldier woke up. He saw a woman in a white robe, but he could not see her face. "It's ten o'clock," he said.

"Why am I here?" asked La Llorona. "Where are my babies?" Before the soldier could reply, she began to sob and cry. "Where are my children?" she asked again. "Help me find my babies," she begged. Then she disappeared.

The soldier did not know what to do or say. He looked around for her, but she was gone. The poor man was very afraid.

"Who is she?" he wondered. "Where did she go?" He stood alone, looking into the darkness. He was terrified. Every time something moved, he felt more frightened.

After a long time another soldier came. "What's the matter?" the second soldier asked. "You look very scared. You look as though you've seen a ghost."

The first soldier tried to speak. He could not! His voice was silent. He tried again. At last he was able to say, in a small voice, "Perhaps, I have seen a phantom." He stood close to the other man. He was very glad to be with somebody else. "I was standing here, when a woman came and spoke to me. She asked me, 'Where are my babies?' Then she disappeared."

"That's La Llorona," the second soldier said. "She drowned her children. Now she's looking for them."

"I'm going to tell the officer in charge about her," the first soldier said.

"Don't bother," the second soldier advised him. "I'm telling you, he doesn't believe that story."

But the first soldier went to the officer and told his story. "...and then, she disappeared," he said. "She just vanished. I looked for her, but she wasn't there."

The officer laughed. "A lot of men tell me that story," he said. "I think you were drunk. Don't touch any more tequila. Then you won't imagine things that don't happen. I don't believe that people can disappear."

The soldier went away but he was still afraid. The officer walked through the city. He passed by the church of Santa Anita. There was nobody in the street. He felt very lonely. Then he thought he saw somebody. "Good," he thought, "I'm tired of being alone." He hurried forward. He wanted to speak to the person. He saw that it was a woman. She was wearing a white robe. He could not see her face.

"Why are you out by yourself, my pretty lady?" he asked. "Let me take you to a safe place. It's dangerous for you to be alone."

The woman did not speak. She kept walking. Her veil hid her face. She was silent.

The officer tried to speak to her, but still she did not reply. At last he said, "Who are you, my good lady? Please let me see your face."

The woman did not turn.

The officer laughed. "My men tell me about a strange woman who can vanish. They say she can disappear." He began to feel afraid. "Are you that person? Are you La Llorona?"

The woman turned to him. She drew back her veil. She had no skin on her face. All he could see was her skull. Her face was all bones.

"Where are my children?" she asked.

The officer fell to the ground. The next day some people found him. He mumbled, "La Llorona! La Llorona!" He was afraid of anyone who came near him. A few days later, he died.

Everyone talked about La Llorona. Every night, at about ten o'clock, the people could hear a woman crying and wailing, "Where are my babies? Where are my children?"

All Mexico City was afraid. Nobody went out after ten o'clock. People stayed in their homes and listened to La Llorona's terrible weeping and crying. The sound of weeping was loudest in Plaza Mayor, in the middle of the city.

One night La Llorona came to the center of the square. She knelt down, facing the east. She put her head to the ground and cried for a long time. Then, she left the city. She disappeared and nobody ever saw her again.

But people have heard her. And when the wind blows, people say that it is La Llorona, looking for her children. ▲

UNDERSTANDING WHAT YOU READ

Answer the following questions.

1. What was La Llorona looking for?
2. What happened to the officer?

VOCABULARY

A. *Read the sentences. Circle the letter of the correct meanings for the underlined words. Use the meanings from the story.*

1. La Llorona took her new, little baby son to the <u>canal</u> outside Mexico City.

   a. something with water in it

   b. something dry

   c. something bad

2. She held him under water until he <u>drowned</u>.

   a. died from too much sun

   b. lived for a long time

   c. died because he could not breathe under water

3. Then, she <u>disappeared</u>. The soldier did not know what to do or say. He looked around for her, but she was not there anymore.

   a. was sad about something

   b. heard about something

   c. was not seen anymore

4. "My men tell me about a strange woman who can <u>vanish</u>."

   a. disappear

   b. become visible

   c. see very far

5. It's dangerous for you to be <u>alone</u>.

   a. by yourself

   b. with La Llorona

   c. a woman

B. Write your own sentences using the words below.

canal _____

_____

drowning _____

_____

disappear _____

_____

alone _____

_____

DISCUSSION

1. Why do you think La Llorona killed her children?
2. What do we know about the children's father? What sort of man was he?

TELL IT YOUR WAY

A. *Do you know any stories like this one? If so, tell the story to the class. If you do not know any other stories, work with your classmates to make up a story.*

B. *Pretend you are La Llorona. Tell your story to the class.*

DICTATION

_____

_____

_____

_____

_____

THE HIDDEN GOLD MINE

BEFORE YOU READ

Answer the following questions.

1. What is a gold mine?
2. Have you ever been to a gold mine?
3. Where are gold mines located?
4. Do you want to be a miner? Why? Why not?
5. What do you see in the illustration?

USING WHAT YOU KNOW

Find the meaning for each word. Then write the letters of the correct meanings on the lines.

__b__	1. shouted	a. worried about something
_____	2. whispered	b. said very loudly
_____	3. exclaimed	c. said again
_____	4. repeated	d. said very quietly
_____	5. fretted	e. said in a very excited way

nce upon a time there was a rich man named Quintana. He was a very greedy merchant. Quintana bought gold from the Indians. He paid very little money for the gold. Then he sold it for a lot of money.

Quintana became very, very rich. He had a great fortune. Nobody in the city of Tepec had more money than Quintana. He had enough money to last for the rest of his life.

But Quintana was never satisfied. He always wanted more. He wanted all the gold, and he wanted to know where the mine was.

One day an old Indian was in Quintana's shop. Quintana was buying the man's gold.

"Will you take me to your mine?" Quintana asked the old man.

"What's that you say?" the old man asked.

"Will you take me to your gold mine?" Quintana repeated.

"Eh?" the old man said. He put his hand behind his ear.

"Will you take me to your mine?" Quintana shouted.

"No need to shout," the old man said. "I'm only a little bit deaf. I can still hear all right if you speak clearly."

Quintana took a deep breath and said very slowly and very clearly, "Will — you — take — me — to — your — mine?"

The old man looked at him for a long time. Then he spat on the floor.

"You must think I'm stupid," he said. "No. I'm not a fool. I won't take you to my gold mine." And he walked straight out of the shop.

Quintana stayed in his shop. Every time an Indian came to sell gold, Quintana asked, "Will you take me to your gold mine?"

One day Quintana was buying gold from two young Indians. "Will you take me to the mine where you found this gold?" he asked.

One of the men looked very angry. "I want you to know something about gold," he said. "Poor people work hard to find gold. Simple people like us work in gold mines, and rich men like you make money from the gold mines. No! I will not take you to the mine."

Quintana could see that nobody wanted to take him to the gold. He wondered how he could get to the money. Then he had an idea.

There was a priest in the little town. He looked after the poor and the sick. "The people love the priest," Quintana said to himself. "They trust him. They believe he is a good man. They will give him anything they can."

Quintana walked to the priest's house. He took off his hat and bowed to the priest. "Father, " he said humbly, like a poor man, "I need your help."

The priest sighed. He knew Quintana. He was the richest man in the town, but he would not give the church any money. "Come in, my son," he said. He led Quintana into the house.

"I have an idea that will make money for your holy work," Quintana said. He put his head close to the priest and whispered, "I can get gold for the church."

The priest was amazed. He looked at Quintana. "You spoke very quietly, my son," he said. "Did I hear you right? Can you get gold for the church?"

"Yes," Quintana said. "If you help me, I can."

"What do I have to do?" the priest asked.

"I want you to find out where the Indians have their gold mines" Quintana replied.

"Why don't you ask them yourself?" the priest asked.

"They won't tell me," Quintana said. "They don't trust me. But they trust you. They will show you the mine. Then you can tell me where it is."

"No," the priest said. "I don't think that's a good idea. You'll just go and steal the gold. Then the Indians will have nothing."

"Father," Quintana said, "I will give you half the money that I get from the gold in the mine. You can help your people."

The priest looked out of his house to the north. An old woman was carrying water from the river. She looked tired. He looked to the west; a few miserable hens scratched in the dust. He looked to the south, and he saw hungry children. He looked to the east. A ragged man limped by. One of his legs was shorter than the other.

"You could help all those people," Quintana said. "All you have to do is tell me one thing. Tell me where the gold mine is. If you do that, you will have money for your people. If you do not, they will just get poorer and poorer."

Quintana walked away quickly.

The poor priest fretted and worried. What could he do? He tried to sleep, but it was impossible. He thought of all the things he could do for his people if he had a little money.

After many sleepless nights, the priest went to Quintana.

"All right," the priest said. "You win. I will find out where the gold mine is. I will ask the Indians."

When the priest asked the Indians, "Where is your gold mine?" they smiled at him.

"We can't tell you that, Father," they said.

"Please show me the mine," the priest begged. "I just want to know that one thing."

The Indians talked for a long time. At last, one of them said, "All right, Father, we'll take you to the mine. But you must wear a blindfold. We won't let you see how we get to the mine. We'll wrap a cloth around your eyes. And we'll give you a donkey to ride."

The priest agreed. After the Indians went away, he went to see Quintana.

"They will take me to the mine," he said. "But they'll cover my eyes."

"How will you find your way back?" Quintana asked.

"I am going to take a bag of corn with me," the priest replied. "I will put a little hole in the bag, so the corn will fall out. It will rain soon, and the corn will grow. We can follow the corn to the mine."

"That's a wonderful idea," Quintana exclaimed. He was very excited. "Each grain of corn will grow," he thought. "Then the corn will lead us to the mine. It will be like a green road."

The next day the Indians came to the priest's house. They covered his eyes and put him on a donkey. Then they led his donkey. He could feel the corn dropping out of the bag.

When they got to the mine, the Indians took off the priest's blindfold. "Here it is," they said proudly. "This is our gold mine."

The priest looked around him. All the Indians were smiling. One man said, "Father, you are a good priest. Here is some gold for the church."

The priest took it. Tears came to his eyes. How could he cheat these people? How could he let Quintana find the mine?

Then another man said, "Father, I saw some corn dropping out of your bag."

The priest was afraid. He opened his mouth and shut it again.

"Don't worry, Father," the man said. "You didn't lose it. I picked up every grain. It's in this new bag."

The Indian smiled and handed the priest a bag full of corn. ▲

UNDERSTANDING WHAT YOU READ

Put these events in the correct order. Write 1 by the first event. Write 6 by the last event.

___5___   1. The priest rode a donkey to the mine.

_____   2. Quintana visited the priest.

_____   3. The man gave the priest his corn.

_____   4. Quintana asked the old man to take him to the mine.

_____   5. The young man refused to take Quintana to the mine.

_____   6. The priest agreed to help Quintana.

VOCABULARY

A. *Read the sentences. Circle the letter of the correct meaning for the underlined words. Use the meanings from the story.*

1. Quintana became very, very rich. He had <u>a great fortune</u>.
   - a. good luck
   - b. lots of money
   - c. misfortune

2. But Quintana wanted more. He <u>was very greedy</u>. He wanted all the gold.
   - a. wanted everything
   - b. was old
   - c. was tired

3. "You must think I'm <u>stupid</u>," he said. "No, I'm not a fool. I won't take you to my mine."
   - a. very clever
   - b. very foolish
   - c. very rich

4. <u>Simple</u> people like us work in gold mines.
   - a. clever
   - b. rich
   - c. poor and uneducated

5. Quintana took off his hat and bowed to the priest. "Father," he said <u>humbly</u> like a poor man. "I need your help."

    a. proudly

    b. rudely

    c. modestly

6. A ragged man <u>limped</u> by. One of his legs was shorter than the other.

    a. walked unevenly

    b. ran

    c. walked quickly

B. Write your own sentences using the words and phrases below.

a great fortune _____

_____

stupid _____

_____

limped _____

_____

DISCUSSION

1. Will the priest be able to find his way back to the mine?
2. What do you think the priest told Quintana when he returned to the village?

TELL IT YOUR WAY

Choose part of the story and draw a picture of it. You may use stick figures. Explain your drawing to the class.

PEDRO DE URDEMALAS AND THE MAGIC COOKING POT

BEFORE YOU READ

Answer the following questions.

1. What do you know about Pedro de Urdemalas?
2. How do you make a fire?
3. What words do you think of when you think about fire?
4. What do you see in the illustration?

USING WHAT YOU KNOW

Circle the words that describe Pedro.

clever	honest	trickster	liar
stupid	helpful	kind	victim

edro de Urdemalas had no money. All he had in the world was a handful of beans and a cooking pot.

"Perhaps if I sell the pot..." he thought. He looked at it. The pot was old and dirty. Nobody would buy it.

Pedro sat down and thought for a long time. He had an idea. He sat and thought a lot longer. His idea was growing. Then it was a plan.

Pedro got up and picked up his pot. He found the biggest road out of the town. He walked along it.

Pedro traveled for about two hours. Then he crossed a small river. He filled his pot with water and traveled a little farther. He wanted to find a safe place to stop. At last he found a good spot.

Pedro looked up and down the road. He could see if anyone was coming from any direction. This was a good place for his plan.

Pedro gathered wood for a fire. He worked quickly. Soon he had a hot fire burning. He put heavy wood on it so that it would burn for a long time. Then he dug a hole next to the fire.

He looked up and down the road. Still nobody was coming. Pedro put the beans into the pot. Then he put the pot on the fire. Soon the water began to boil. The beans smelled good.

Pedro looked up and down the road again. He could see someone approaching. Pedro smiled; his victim was coming.

Pedro worked quickly. He pushed the fire into the hole and put the pot on top of it. The fire was out of sight. The beans kept boiling. Pedro sat down beside his pot, and began to eat the beans very slowly.

The stranger came up to where Pedro was sitting. He watched Pedro carefully pick up the cooked beans with a long stick.

"It's much too hot to put my fingers in the pot," Pedro said.

The stranger looked at the pot. "What is making that pot boil?" he asked.

Pedro smiled at him. He looked up and down the road, as though he wanted to see if anyone was coming. "This is a magic pot," he whispered. "As soon as I put the food in it, the pot will boil by itself. I don't have to make a fire."

"That's wonderful!" the stranger exclaimed. "I'm on the road a lot. I need a pot just like that. Will you sell it? How much do you want for it?"

"Hush!" Pedro said. "This is a magic pot. Don't let it hear you talk like that!"

The stranger whispered, "I want to buy the pot. How much is it?"

Pedro looked very sad. "I need the money," he said, "so I'll let you buy it for a thousand dollars. But be quiet about it. If the pot hears that I am selling it, it will be angry. Sit down with it. Don't move at all until you can't see me any more. Then the pot won't know that you own it."

"All right," the stranger said. "It's a lot of money, but a pot like that is very valuable."

The stranger gave Pedro the money. Pedro took it.

"Now, be very quiet," Pedro said. "Don't let the pot know that I have gone."

Pedro crept quietly away. The traveler sat silently with the pot for nearly an hour. He noticed that the beans were no longer boiling. "I wonder why it stopped," he thought. He picked up the pot and saw the ashes of the fire underneath it.

"I've been fooled!" he yelled. "Wait until I get my hands on that little rascal!" He was furious. He started to run after Pedro. But Pedro was too far away.

Then he thought, "What if other people find out how stupid I've been? They will all laugh at me. No, I'll be quiet about it. I won't tell anybody."

So the stranger went on his way, a sadder but wiser man. But Pedro laughed and went into another town. Now he had a thousand dollars. He had money to live on until his next trick.   ▲

UNDERSTANDING WHAT YOU READ

Put these events in the correct order. Write 1 by the first event. Write 6 by the last event.

___1___ 1. Pedro had no money.

_____ 2. Pedro crept away with one thousand dollars.

_____ 3. Pedro pushed the fire into the hole.

_____ 4. The stranger bought the pot from Pedro.

_____ 5. Pedro made a big fire.

_____ 6. Pedro put the pot on the fire in the hole.

VOCABULARY

Read the sentences. Circle the letter of the correct meaning for the underlined words. Use the meanings from the story.

1. <u>All he had in the world</u> was a handful of beans and a cooking pot.

    a. He had lots of other things.

    b. he had the world

    c. he had nothing else

2. He <u>traveled</u> for about two hours.

    a. walked

    b. boiled

    c. crept

3. His <u>victim</u> was coming!

    a. someone who is coming

    b. someone Pedro can trick

    c. someone who will trick Pedro

4. "This is a <u>magic</u> pot," he whispered.

    a. dirty

    b. old

    c. strange and wonderful

5. "This is a magic pot," he <u>whispered</u>.

    a. said softly

    b. said

    c. smiled

6. <u>I'm on the road</u> a lot.

    a. I sleep on the road

    b. I travel

    c. I own the road

7. "I've been fooled!" he <u>yelled</u>.

    a. whispered

    b. shouted loudly

    c. said

DISCUSSION

1. What kind of man was the stranger?
2. Why did the stranger believe Pedro?
3. What advice would you give to the stranger?
4. How did Pedro trick the stranger?

TELL IT YOUR WAY

Draw a wanted poster for Pedro. Describe him. List his crimes. Explain how he tricks people.

DICTATION

_____

_____

_____

_____

_____

_____

THE BOBO RIDES ON A BROOM

BEFORE YOU READ

Answer the following questions.

1. What is a witch?
2. What do you know about witches?
3. What do you see in the illustration?

USING WHAT YOU KNOW

Find the meaning for each word. Then write the letters of the correct meanings on the lines.

__c__	1. wandered	a.	turned while falling
_____	2. cackling	b.	became very still
_____	3. froze	c.	moved around aimlessly
_____	4. spell	d.	part of something
_____	5. share	e.	magic words that make something happen
_____	6. tumbled	f.	making a noise like a hen

bobo is a very stupid person who gets everything wrong.

Once upon a time a bobo went into the forest to gather wood. He didn't have an ax to cut down any trees. He hoped he would just find some wood on the ground. He wandered through the forest, looking at the trees. Soon he forgot why he was in the forest.

He kept wandering among the trees. It was very, very cold, and it was getting colder all the time. He roamed on, moving aimlessly from one place to another.

Then the bobo turned around to go back. He didn't know where to go. He was lost!

The bobo was getting colder and colder by the minute. His teeth chattered with the cold. His nose was like a block of ice. He couldn't even feel his fingers and toes.

At last he came to a small hut in the forest. He knocked on the door, but nobody answered. He knocked again. Then he pushed the door open and went in.

It was very dark in the hut. "This is scary," the bobo thought. "Still, it's better than being outside."

The bobo found a pile of old rags in a corner. He lay down, covered himself, and went to sleep.

He woke at midnight. He could hear people laughing. It was a strange, dry, cackling laugh. He lifted his head and looked around carefully. The moonlight was flooding through a window. It made the floor look white.

The bobo froze in terror. There were twelve old witches sitting at the edge of the moonlit floor. They wore dark gowns and looked like twelve black shadows.

The bobo stayed absolutely still.

The witches stood up. They began to laugh again. Then they began to dance. They danced faster and faster. The first witch took a cup and drank from it. She passed it to her sisters. They all drank and laughed some more.

The bobo crept further under his pile of old rags.

"I mustn't let them find me," he thought. "I've heard stories about witches. Sometimes they turn people into birds, or animals, or even snakes."

So he stayed in his hiding place, but he was very curious. He put his head up carefully to see what was happening.

After a while the witches stopped drinking. One of them picked up a broom. She sat comfortably on it and said, "Fly me faster than a fairy — without God, without Saint Mary!" With a whoosh! she flew out the window.

The other witches followed her. They flew away, one after the other. They looked like big bats in the light of the moon. Then they flew higher, until the bobo could not see them anymore.

"I wish I could do that," the bobo said. He came out from his hiding place and looked around the room. He found an old blanket and a broom.

He looked at the broom for a long time. "I wonder..." he thought. He picked it up. Then he put it down again.

Finally he made up his mind. He wrapped himself in the blanket. He sat on the broom and said, "Fly me faster than a fairy — without God, without Saint Mary!"

Whoosh! The broom carried him out of the window. He flew through the air like a great bird. He soared above the trees and flew through the clouds.

"I like this," he thought. He said again, "Fly me faster than a fairy — without God, without Saint Mary!" The broom flew higher and faster. The bobo laughed with pleasure.

"I want to do this more," he cried out. "Fly me faster than a fairy — fly with God and good Saint Mary!"

The broom stopped, and the bobo fell through the air. He tumbled over and over. He had mixed up the spell. Now he could not think of the magic words.

He was falling toward a fire at the edge of the forest. His big blanket flapped around him. He tried to run on the air, but it was no good.

A group of robbers was sitting around the fire. They were counting their gold.

"The devil loves us," one of the robbers said. "Look how much gold we have."

"Shh!" another robber said. "The devil will hear you and come for his share."

They all laughed. Then they heard a whooshing sound from above them. They looked up. It was the bobo, falling through the air. His old blanket looked like the devil's cape.

"Ho!" cried the bobo. "Make room for me. Let a poor devil land softly."

"You fool!" one robber said to another. "You called the devil!" All the robbers ran away as fast as they could. Some people say they are still running.

The bobo landed in the middle of the pile of treasure. He could not believe his eyes. He picked up the gold coins and bit them to see if they were real. He made a pile of silver coins. He put the necklaces around his neck.

The bobo picked up all the treasure and put it in the middle of a big cloth. He wrapped it all up, to take it home.

He was cold and a little bruised from his fall, but he felt no pain. He took his cloth full of treasure and started to walk. He could see his home through the trees.

So the bobo went home a very happy man. And a very rich one. And nobody ever saw the robbers again. ▲

UNDERSTANDING WHAT YOU READ

A. Answer the questions below.

1. What is a bobo?
2. Why did the bobo fall?
3. Why did the robbers run away?
4. Why was the bobo afraid of witches?

B. Put these events in the correct order. Write 1 by the first event. Write 7 by the last event.

___2___ 1. The bobo hid in a hut and went to sleep.

_____ 2. The bobo flew on a broom, but he forgot the magic spell.

_____ 3. The bobo woke up and saw some witches in the room.

_____ 4. The bobo fell through the air into a pile of treasure.

_____ 5. The bobo was lost in the forest.

_____ 6. The robbers ran away.

_____ 7. The witches flew out the window.

VOCABULARY

Write words and phrases from the story that have the same meaning as the underlined words and phrases.

1. <u>collect</u> wood   _gather_ _____

2. His teeth <u>bumped together</u>. _____

3. This is <u>frightening</u>. _____

4. Moonlight was <u>spreading like water</u>. _____

5. He <u>wanted very much to see</u>. _____

6. He <u>decided</u>. _____

7. He <u>flew high above</u> the trees. _____

8. It was <u>useless</u>. _____

9. His big blanket <u>waved wildly</u>. _____

10. The bobo <u>stopped falling</u>. _____

DISCUSSION

1. If someone called you a bobo, how would you feel?
2. Do you think the bobo was lucky? Why?
3. Do you think he deserved his good fortune?

TELL IT YOUR WAY

A. Tell any other stories you know about stupid people like the bobo. If you do not know any other stories, work with your partner or classmates to make up a story.

B. Work with a partner. Pretend you are the bobo and tell your story.

PEDRO DE URDEMALAS SELLS A TREE

BEFORE YOU READ

Answer the following questions.

1. Who is Pedro de Urdemalas?
2. What do you expect to happen in this story?
3. Will Pedro help the people in this story? Why? Why not?
4. Will Pedro trick the people? If so, how will he trick them?
5. Look at the man on the right. Why would you be afraid of him?
6. How did Pedro put the coin on the tree?
7. What do you see in the illustration?

USING WHAT YOU KNOW

There are seven words in this puzzle. Two have been found for you. Find five more words.

```
V   Q   S   A   I   D   B
N   I   C   E   H   L   H
A   M   A   Z   E   D   O
V   T   R   H   F   G   L
F   I   E   R   C   E   E
U   Q   D   L   T   S   P
```

 n our last story about Pedro, he sold a man an old cooking pot. Pedro tricked the man. The man thought the pot boiled without a fire. So he bought it from Pedro for a thousand dollars.

Pedro ran down the road until he was far away from that man and the pot. He ran until he was exhausted. He was so tired he couldn't run anymore. At last he decided it was safe to stop running. He walked to a tree close to the road and sat down to rest.

He could feel an idea growing in his head. "It would be nice to have another one thousand dollars," he thought. He took a coin from his pocket and looked at it for a long time. Then he made a hole in it.

Pedro looked up and down the road. There was no one in sight. He was very clever. He hung the coin carefully on the tree. The coin looked as though it was growing on the branch. Then he lay back and went to sleep.

The next day, two men were traveling up the road. They were amazed when they saw the shining gold coin growing on the branch of the tree. They hurried to the tree to pick the strange fruit.

Pedro was waiting for them. "Hey," he yelled. "Leave my tree alone."

"What sort of tree is it?" one of the men asked.

Pedro looked very fierce, so they backed away from him. "It's a special gold-bearing tree," Pedro said. "It bears twice a year. This is the first fruit of this season's crop." He stood in front of the tree as though he was trying to protect it.

"How much will you sell it for?" one of the men asked.

"Do you take me for a fool?" Pedro replied. "Why would I sell a wonderful tree like this?"

The two men stood in front of Pedro and looked at him in a nasty way. Pedro began to feel afraid.

One of the men had a big knife in his belt. "We won't leave until you sell the tree to us," he said.

"All right, all right!" Pedro said. "Have it your way. I want two thousand dollars and the fruit you can see."

The man rubbed his knife. "I'll give you five hundred dollars," he said.

"I want one thousand dollars and the fruit. I'm only selling the tree because I like you."

"It's a deal," the man said.

Pedro took the gold coin. He was very glad to leave. He didn't like the look of that man with the knife.

The two fools came and lived near the tree. They watered it and looked after it. They even slept under it. They searched it every morning and every afternoon. They looked for gold coins every day for an entire year. Of course, they never found one. Then at last, they realized that Pedro had fooled them. But it was too late. He was far, far away.

Pedro kept traveling on. Perhaps he is still on his travels. ▲

UNDERSTANDING WHAT YOU READ

Match these sentences. Write the correct letters on the line.

    e   1. Pedro fooled people and took their money.

            2. Pedro hung the coin carefully on the tree.

            3. The men looked at Pedro in a nasty way.

            4. The men saw the gold coin growing on the tree.

            5. Pedro ran until he was exhausted.

            6. The men looked after the tree for an entire year.

a. He was tired.

b. He was scared.

c. He was clever.

d. They were fooled.

e. He was a thief.

f. They were amazed.

VOCABULARY

Write words and phrases from the story that have the same meanings as the underlined words and phrases.

1. <u>very tired</u>   *exhausted*

2. They were <u>surprised</u>. _____

3. <u>pluck</u> the strange fruit _____

4. Pedro looked very <u>frightening</u>. _____

5. It <u>has fruit</u> twice a year. _____

6. trying to <u>save it from them</u> _____

7. Do you <u>think I'm stupid</u>? _____

8. In <u>an unpleasant manner</u> _____

9. <u>Do as you like</u>. _____

10. <u>We agree</u>. _____

DISCUSSION

A. Answer the following questions.

1. How do you feel about this story?
2. Are you angry with Pedro? Why? Why not?
3. Do you feel sorry for the two men? Why? Why not?

B. Complete the grid below with your group or partner. Decide which words describe each person. Put yes if the word describes the person. Put no if the word does not describe the person. Put 0 if you don't know if it describes the person.

	clever	honest	kind	rich	happy	frightening	funny
Pedro	yes	no					
The men who bought the tree							
The man with the knife					O		

TELL IT YOUR WAY

A. In your own words, tell your partner or classmates the story, "Pedro de Urdemalas Sells a Tree."

B. Make another ending to this story. Pretend the men don't believe Pedro's story. What do you think would happen?

C. Draw the different parts of the story on a board. With your classmates, decide how many pictures you will need.

D. Work with your classmates. Act out the story without speaking.

FOOL'S DAY

BEFORE YOU READ

Answer the following questions.

1. What do you know about Fool's Day?
2. What day is Fool's Day in your country?
3. What do people do on Fool's Day?
4. How can you tell that someone is proud?
5. What do you see in the illustration?

USING WHAT YOU KNOW

Find the meaning for each word. Then write the letters of the correct meanings on the lines.

__c__	1. advice	a. sneaked, walked very quietly
_____	2. beat	b. three hundred years
_____	3. three centuries	c. help and suggestions
_____	4. naughty	d. young people
_____	5. youths	e. mischievous
_____	6. crept	f. bend over to show respect
_____	7. bow	g. hit, punish

ur story is about a proud man who lived in Colombia 300 years ago. His name was Don Ramiro.

Don Ramiro loved to tell people how important his family was. He told people that the kings of Spain always asked his family for advice. Perhaps the king would do nothing without asking Don Ramiro's family for their help!

"You see, my dear," Don Ramiro told his wife, "my family is very important. Think of it. We are powerful in Spain. And Spain is the greatest country in the world!"

He boasted about his family to everyone he met.

"Is it true that you are part of the family of the new Spanish viceroy of Granada?" a man asked him. Granada was the name of Colombia three centuries ago. The viceroy was the ruler sent by the king of Spain to rule Granada.

Don Ramiro smiled mysteriously. He didn't say yes and he didn't say no. But he put a portrait of the viceroy in his house. Don Ramiro often stood near the picture. People could see that he looked like the viceroy.

Don Ramiro was a proud man. He was boastful and sometimes foolish, but he was not a bad man. He was very respectable. He was honest. He gave to charity, and he was kind to the poor. He was, however, a man that people loved to trick. He had a very hard time every Fool's Day.

The same thing happened every year. On the night of December 27, naughty children and youths gathered near Don Ramiro's home. They waited for the cathedral clock to chime at midnight. At last they heard the bell — one, two, three, four, five, six, seven, eight, nine, ten, eleven, twelve. Then it was December 28, Fool's Day.

They ran to Don Ramiro's house and beat on the door.

Don Ramiro sat up in bed. "What can be the matter?" he thought. "Is somebody hurt? Is there a war?" He hurried to the window and looked out.

"Fool!" the young men and children cried out.

Don Ramiro was furious. "You rude, naughty children!" he cried. "Do you know who I am? Don't you have any respect for me and for my name? Your parents should beat you. Wait there for me to punish you!"

Of course, they all laughed and ran away. Don Ramiro was very upset. He went back to his room and told his wife all about the mischievous children.

"There, there," Doña Teresa said. "Good husband, this is Fool's Day. They'll play tricks all over town. Let's forget about it."

So Don Ramiro let his wife lead him back to bed.

A year passed. It was midnight of December 27 again. Don Ramiro was asleep in his bed when he heard a great noise outside his house.

"What can that be?" he wondered. Then he remembered. It was Fool's Day. He sneaked to his window and looked down at the door. He could see a small group of people. "I'll teach them," he thought.

He looked around for something to throw at the people. There was a flower pot in the corner of the room. It contained a big plant with bright red flowers. Don Ramiro picked it up and crept to the window. He opened the window. "Fool!" the young people cried.

Don Ramiro threw the pot at them. They all jumped aside, and the pot broke on the ground. The young people ran away, laughing.

Don Ramiro went back to bed.

"I heard something break," his wife said. "What was it?"

"Just a flower pot," Don Ramiro said. "I threw it at the tricksters."

Doña Teresa looked angry. "What color were the flowers in the pot?" she asked.

"They were red," Don Ramiro said.

Doña Teresa was pale with anger. "That was my best plant," she said. "I spent a whole year growing those flowers." She turned her back on Don Ramiro.

Another year passed. Don Ramiro got ready for Fool's Day. He prepared a long speech and waited for midnight. At last he heard the bell—one, two, three, four, five, six, seven, eight, nine, ten, eleven, twelve.

He opened the door just as the tricksters began to knock on it. Before they could say anything, he began to read. "To the people of the good city of Tunja . . ."

Everyone stopped to listen. Don Ramiro went on, "Know that you are angering a great man. I, Don Ramiro, am part of a fine family. We have . . ."

He stopped. He saw that some people were laughing quietly. He tried to speak again, but people were laughing out loud. Some of them were shaking with laughter. They were laughing so hard they could hardly say "Fool."

Don Ramiro slammed his door. He was hurt and angry.

Another year passed. On December 27, Don Ramiro left his house to walk around the town. He was carrying a very large shotgun. He went to the town square where people were getting water from the well.

Don Ramiro stood at the top of some stairs and said, "Do you all see this huge shotgun? I will shoot at anyone who comes to my door tonight."

Don Ramiro marched down the steps and away before anyone could speak to him. He went all around the town, showing people his shotgun. At last he came home, tired but happy.

"Nobody will come here tonight," he told Doña Teresa. "They all know that I will shoot them. Now they know that they must treat me with respect."

"I'm sure they do, my dear," Doña Teresa said.

Doña Teresa and Don Ramiro went to bed peacefully. Midnight passed, and nobody came.

At one o'clock, Don Ramiro awoke to the sound of a horse outside. He peeped through his window. A beautiful white horse stood under the light in the courtyard. A noble looking man, dressed in the uniform of an army officer, was looking at Don Ramiro's house. The officer had a large envelope in his hand.

Don Ramiro went downstairs to open his door. He left his shotgun where he could reach it. "What do you want?" he asked coldly.

The officer came forward and bowed low. "Do I have the honor of addressing Don Ramiro Quesada Vazquez de Vega?" he asked in a loud, clear voice.

Don Ramiro bowed and said, "You do!"

"Are you truly Don Ramiro Quesada Vazquez de Vega, of the great Ramiro Quesada Vazquez de Vega family, advisers to the kings of Spain?" the officer asked again. He spoke loudly, like an actor on a stage. Then he bowed again.

"The same!" Don Ramiro replied, bowing.

"Don Ramiro Quesada Vazquez de Vega, relative of the viceroy?" the officer enquired.

"I am he," Don Ramiro said. "How can I help you, sir?"

The officer bowed yet again. "I have a letter for you from His Excellency the Viceroy," he said. "Will you receive it?"

"Of course," Don Ramiro said. The officer bowed deeply and handed Don Ramiro the large envelope. Then he mounted his horse and rode quickly away.

The envelope was hard to open. Don Ramiro moved under the light. He tore the envelope and found a large piece of paper. There were two words in the middle of the page. They were very, very small. It was hard to see them.

Don Ramiro moved closer to the light. He stood in the middle of his courtyard and read "Poor fool!" And as he read, he could hear people laughing in the dark. ▲

UNDERSTANDING WHAT YOU READ

Circle the words that best complete the sentences.

Don Ramiro was a very (proud, pretty, strong) man. He talked a lot about his (flower pot, money, family). The young people loved to (listen to, trick, look at) him on Fool's Day. Don Ramiro was very (pleased, angry, tired) when he was tricked.

One day, the tricksters made Don Ramiro think he had a (horse, letter, chair) from the viceroy. Then he read the letter, it said (Dear sir, Poor fool, My friend).

VOCABULARY

Look back through the story to find words and phrases that describe Don Ramiro. Then write a description of Don Ramiro.

proud _____

_____

_____

_____

_____

TELL IT YOUR WAY

A. *Pretend you are Don Ramiro. You are in the middle of the courtyard with the letter that says "Poor fool." You can hear people laughing. What can you do?*

B. *Tell the class about Fool's Day (or a day like it) in your native country.*

C. *How do you think Doña Teresa felt when "the officer" tricked Don Ramiro?*

D. *Pretend you are Doña Teresa. Tell the story to a friend.*

THE SHARK HUNTER

BEFORE YOU READ

Answer the following questions.

1. What do you know about sharks?
2. Have you ever seen a shark?
3. What is a medallion?
4. Why would a medallion make someone feel safe?
5. What do you see in the illustration?

USING WHAT YOU KNOW

Think of all the words you know that relate to a shark. Then write the words below.

_____

_____

his story is about a brave man named Rufino. He was a hunter of sharks. He lived in Puerto Rico, long ago, when Spain still ruled large parts of Latin America.

Rufino often fought the sharks that came into the Bay of Aguada. It was a beautiful place — calm and serene — but people did not dare to swim or fish for very long because of the great sharks.

Some of these horrible fish were more than twelve feet long. They had rows of sharp teeth, and they could swim faster than any other creature. One bite of their mighty jaws could remove a man's arm.

Everyone wondered how Rufino dared to fight such monsters. It was because Rufino was not only brave and strong, but he was also pious and faithful to the church. His girlfriend, Maria, gave him a medallion of the Virgin Carmen. He always wore this medallion on a chain around his neck when he went shark hunting. The medallion made him feel safe.

One day Rufino went to meet Maria on the beach. She ran forward to embrace him.

"Where is your medallion, Rufino?" Maria asked.

Rufino put his hand to his neck. The medallion was not there. He became very pale. "I've lost it!" he cried. "How can I hunt for sharks now? The Virgin Carmen will not protect me!"

"Hush!" Maria said. "She knows you are a good man. She will protect you."

But now Rufino was afraid to go shark hunting. Many months passed. Rufino didn't go shark hunting. He barely made a living doing odd jobs. He was very unhappy. He wanted to marry Maria, but he did not have enough money. He was afraid he would never earn enough for a wedding.

Then, one day, the Spanish viceroy and the Bishop of Puebla sailed into Aguada. People rushed to greet them. The viceroy was a very important man. He was the governor sent by the King of Spain. The bishop was the head of the Roman Catholic church in Puebla.

The viceroy stepped ashore. He looked pale and frightened.

"We have just seen the most horrible creature!" he said. "It was a shark. I'm sure it was at least fifteen feet long. It bumped against the side of the boat. I could see its terrible white teeth."

Everyone nodded. They knew how a shark can scare a man, even a man in a big boat.

"We dare not fish or swim in these waters," a man said. "The sharks will kill us. Now we can only fish from a boat. Our children can't play in the water."

"What can we do?" the bishop asked. He, too, was afraid. "I want someone to kill that shark."

The viceroy agreed.

"We could ask Rufino to fight the shark," a man said. " Rufino is an Indian who lives in our village. He has hunted sharks before." He ran to find Rufino.

"Will you fight the shark?" the people asked. "The viceroy and the bishop are here and they would like to see you kill the creature."

Rufino looked down at the ground. "I'm sorry," he said. "I can't fight sharks anymore. I've lost my medallion of the Virgin Carmen. I can't fight without it."

"I'll give you an ounce of Spanish gold if you kill the shark," the viceroy said.

"And I will give you eight pesos," the bishop added.

Rufino thought about the money. He knew he could marry Maria if he fought the shark, but he was afraid to fight without his medallion. Then he remembered Maria saying, "The Virgin Carmen knows you are a good man. She will protect you."

"All right," Rufino said. "I will fight the shark tomorrow." And he hurried away from the beach.

Rufino could not rest. When he fell asleep, he had bad dreams — dreams where he could not hurt the shark.

When the dawn came, Rufino went to the beach. Everyone was there. The bishop and the viceroy stood together. Maria stood away from the crowd. She was pale and wide eyed and her lips moved slowly as she prayed quietly.

Rufino made the sign of the cross and went into the water. He swam out to meet the shark.

He did not have to wait very long. Soon he saw an evil gray shape coming toward him. It was a huge shark, the biggest he had ever seen. Rufino felt very calm. He knew what he had to do.

The shark swam lazily around him once. Then it came around again. Suddenly, it turned and swam straight at him.

Rufino held his knife ready. As the shark came forward, he moved aside and jabbed the dagger hard into the shark's side. The shark turned quickly and caught Rufino's shoulder with its teeth. Rufino felt his skin tear. He was hurt.

Maria stood on the beach. She could see blood on the water. She was terrified. She was afraid that Rufino was dead.

The shark circled again. Rufino held the knife strongly. The shark rushed toward him and Rufino buried his dagger in the old wound on the shark's side. Then he turned and swam for the shore. He expected the shark to catch him at any minute.

The people pulled him from the water. They were very relieved to see he was alive.

"I'm not strong enough," he gasped. "I can't kill it."

The people quickly bandaged Rufino's shoulder. Then Maria shouted, "Rufino, you did kill the shark. Look! It's floating on the water! Only dead sharks float."

Everyone cheered. The bishop thanked God for letting Rufino kill the shark. He was very grateful. Then the bishop and the viceroy gave Rufino the money they had promised him. The people passed around a hat and put money into it, too. Everyone praised Rufino and said that he was a very brave man.

Later, Maria and Rufino counted the money in the hat. They could get married!

The entire town celebrated Rufino and Maria's wedding. ▲

UNDERSTANDING WHAT YOU READ

A. Answer the questions below.

1. Why was Rufino afraid?
2. Why did Rufino fight the shark, even though he was afraid? (Give two reasons.)

B. Put these events in the correct order. Write 1 by the first event. Write 6 by the last event.

___2___ 1. Rufino lost his medallion.

_____ 2. Rufino and Maria got married.

_____ 3. Rufino killed the shark.

_____ 4. Maria gave Rufino a medallion.

_____ 5. The viceroy asked Rufino to fight the shark.

_____ 6. Rufino fought the shark without the medallion.

C. Tell if each statement is true, false, or maybe could be true. Write true, false, or maybe on the lines. Explain your answers to the class.

false 1. The viceroy was happy when the shark bumped into his boat.

_____ 2. Rufino had pleasant dreams the night before he fought the shark.

_____ 3. Rufino felt very calm when he started to fight the shark.

_____ 4. Maria was very afraid when she saw the blood on the water.

_____ 5. Everyone was relieved when Rufino killed the shark.

VOCABULARY

Complete the crossword puzzle. Use words from the story.

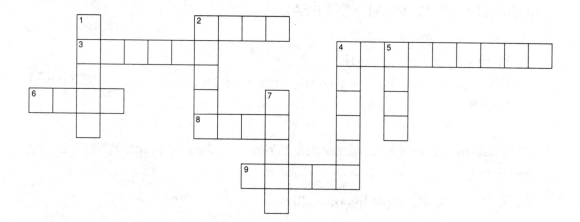

Across

2. to cut with the teeth
3. someone who hunts
4. something you wear for luck, or for protection from harm
6. be brave enough to do something
8. very bad, wicked
9. to have a wedding

Down

1. a big fish with sharp teeth that can kill people
2. very courageous
4. very big and strong
5. the beginning of the day
7. lie on top of the water

TELL IT YOUR WAY

A. *How do you think each person felt in the situations below? Tell all the ways they felt. Discuss your answers with your classmates.*

1. the bishop, when he saw the shark bump his boat

   _____

2. the bishop, when the shark was dead

   _____

3. Maria, when she saw Rufino go into the water to fight the shark

   _____

4. Rufino, when he started to fight the shark

   _____

5. Rufino, when he was swimming to shore

   _____

B. *Draw faces of people with the following expressions: frightened, pleased, worried, and relieved — or mime those feelings for your partner.*

C. *Do you know any stories about sharks? If so, tell the story to your partner or class. If you do not know any other stories, work with your partner or classmates to make up a story.*

JUAN DIEGO AND THE VIRGIN OF GUADALUPE

BEFORE YOU READ

Answer the following questions.

1. Have you heard the story of Juan Diego and the Virgin of Guadalupe?
2. What do you see in the illustration?

USING WHAT YOU KNOW

A. *Tell the class what you know about the Virgin of Guadalupe.*
B. *Do you know these words? If not, ask someone for help with the meanings of the words.*

   angel   bishop   church   priest   last rites   cape

ur story began on December 9, 1531. A poor man named Juan Diego was walking to church in Mexico City. When he came to Tepeyac Hill, he stopped suddenly.

"I'm sure I can hear music," he said. "It's wonderful music. Only angels can sing like that." It sounded so beautiful he did not want to leave the place.

Then Juan Diego heard a sweet voice. "Juan Diego," the voice called gently. "Juan Diego, look this way."

Juan turned around to see where the voice was coming from. He saw the Virgin standing on the rocks of Tepeyac Hill.

Juan Diego was very afraid. He looked away from the Virgin and closed his eyes. Then he opened them again. She was still there. She looked as bright as the sun.

The Virgin smiled at him. Juan Diego fell to his knees. "Don't be afraid, my son," the Virgin said in her soft gentle voice.

Juan Diego looked up. The rocks the Virgin stood on were bright as jewels. There was so much light, he was dazzled. He had to look away again.

"I have a task for you, my son," the Virgin said. "I want you to go to the bishop. Tell him to build a church so I may look after my people."

Juan Diego could not speak.

"Tell the bishop I want a church here, on Tepeyac Hill," the Virgin repeated.

Juan Diego nodded. He wanted to speak, but he was still too afraid. Then the Virgin smiled at him, and he felt warm and safe. He opened his mouth to speak to her, but she had gone.

Juan hurried to the church in Mexico City. He wanted to tell the bishop what had happened.

The bishop laughed at him. "Did you go to sleep on the way here?" he asked. "I think you had a dream." The bishop did not listen to Juan Diego.

The next day, Juan Diego went back to Tepeyac Hill. He waited for a few minutes. Then the Virgin appeared.

"The bishop did not believe me," Juan said sadly. "Perhaps you had better find somebody else to talk to him. I am only a poor man. He won't listen to me."

The Virgin said gently, "You are a good man, Juan Diego. Go back and talk to the bishop again. Tell him that I am the mother of all my people. I want to have a church here so I can take care of them."

Juan went back to the church. He had to wait a long time before he could see the bishop.

"I saw the Virgin again," he said. "She told me to come back to you."

The bishop stared at him for a long time. "I don't think you're lying," he said at last. "I will give you a little test. Ask the Virgin to send me a sign. Then I will know that she is really on Tepeyac Hill."

Juan Diego went back the next day to talk to the Virgin. He told her that the bishop wanted something to prove that she was really there. The Virgin thought for a little while. Then she said, "Come back tomorrow. I will have something for the bishop."

The next day Juan was ready to go to Tepeyac Hill to see the Virgin. He was about to leave when he heard his aunt weeping. She hurried up to him.

"Juan, Juan!" his aunt cried. "Your uncle is very sick. Please get a priest. He must have the last rites before he dies."

Juan went to see his uncle. The old man was very weak. First he was hot. Then he was cold. He was making a lot of noise when he breathed.

Juan felt very sad. He hurried off to get the priest. "I can't see the Virgin today," he thought. "I won't be able to go near Tepeyac Hill."

He was halfway to the priest's house when the Virgin appeared. "You do not need the priest," she said. "Your uncle is well again."

Juan was amazed.

"Trust me," the Virgin said. "Now go back to the hill where you first saw me. You will find some roses for the bishop."

Juan went to the hill. Sure enough, there were splendid roses blooming among the cactus. Juan picked some roses. He had never seen flowers there before.

Juan hid the roses in his cape and went to see the bishop. The bishop's servants would not let him in. They laughed at him.

"Here he is again," they sneered. "Do you believe that the Blessed Virgin would appear to him? Go away!" But Juan would not leave. At last they brought the bishop.

The bishop looked annoyed. He was angry that Juan had come back. "What do you have for me?" he snapped.

Juan opened his cape to show the bishop the roses. Everyone gasped in amazement.

"Aren't they beautiful?" Juan asked. "They were blooming among the cactus." Then he realized that nobody was looking at the roses. They were all looking at his old cape. The face of the Virgin of Guadalupe was on the rough cloth.

The bishop knelt down to pray for forgiveness. Then he said, "Quickly, my son, take me to the place. We will build the Virgin of Guadalupe a fine church. And we will put your cape in it, so everyone can see her face."

When Juan got home, he found that his uncle was better, just as the Virgin had promised. ▲

UNDERSTANDING WHAT YOU READ
Answer the following questions.

1. Where did the Virgin of Guadalupe want the church built?
2. Why did the bishop laugh at Juan Diego?
3. Did the bishop build a church for the Virgin of Guadalupe?

VOCABULARY
Write your own sentences using the words below.

angel _____

_____

bishop _____

_____

church _____

_____

last rites _____

_____

priest _____

_____

cape _____

_____

TELL IT YOUR WAY

A. Answer the following questions. Write your answers in complete sentences.

1. How did Juan Diego feel when he first saw the Virgin?

   _____

2. How did he feel when the bishop did not believe him?

   _____

3. How did he feel when he knew his uncle was dying?

   _____

4. How did he feel when he found the roses on the rocks?

   _____

5. How did he feel when he saw the Virgin's face on his cape?

   _____

B. Role play these parts of the story.
   1. When Juan Diego first tells the bishop about the Virgin of Guadalupe.
   2. When Juan Diego takes the roses to the bishop.

C. Do you know any stories like this one? If so, tell the story to your partner or class.

BEWARE OF BALDHEADS

BEFORE YOU READ

Answer the following questions.

1. What does the title mean?
2. Do you like the man on the right? Why? Why not?
3. What is the boy on the left doing?
4. What do you think is in the bag?
5. What do you see in the illustration?

USING WHAT YOU KNOW

Find eight more words in this puzzle. What do they mean?

```
W   A   S   H   E   R   S

H   B   C   F   T   X   M

I   D   C   J   A   G   O

L   Y   L   K   F   V   N

E   J   E   S   C   G   E

M   E   R   R   I   L   Y

A   S   K   U   K   N   D
```

 ne day a man said to his son, "I want you to go into the city to buy a few things for me."

"Yes, father," the boy replied. He was very excited. He didn't go into the big city very often. His father gave him a bag of money, and the son went merrily into the city.

"I think I'll have a look around for a while," he thought. "It's very early. I have lots of time."

He wandered along for a while. Then he thought, "I am silly! It's foolish for me to carry all this money. I might lose it. I'm going to take it to a place where I can leave it safely."

He saw a sign that said, "Casa de Encargos." Casa de Encargos means House of Safekeeping. "That's a good place," he thought. He went into the shop.

"What can I do for you, young man?" the clerk asked.

"Will you look after my money for me while I go to see the city?" the young man asked.

"Of course," the clerk replied. "Have no fear. All your money is quite safe here!"

So the young man left his money and went into the city. He had a great time. After a few hours he came back to the House of Safekeeping.

"May I have my money back?" he asked politely.

"What money?" the clerk asked.

"The money I left here a little while ago," the young man said.

"You left no money here," the clerk said.

"But sir, I did!"

"I've never seen you before in my life," the clerk said. "Now go away and stop wasting my time."

The young man went home feeling very depressed.

"Where are the things I sent you to buy?" his father asked.

"I couldn't get them," the son said. And he told his father how he had left the money with the clerk.

"Well, well!" the father said. "What does this man look like?"

"He's bald, father."

"Is he as bald as I am?" the father asked.

"You're balder than he is," the son replied.

"Good, good!" the father said. He found an old leather bag and put buttons and old metal washers into it. When it was quite full, the father said, "Now we'll go back to the city."

Father and son walked to the city. As they walked, the father told the son what to do. At last they came to the House of Safekeeping. The father went in by himself.

"May I leave my bag of money here?" he asked.

The clerk looked at the big bag in the man's hand. "Of course, sir," he replied. "Have no fear. All your money is quite safe here!" He put out his hand to take the bag.

Just then, the boy came in. "May I have my money back?" the boy asked politely.

The clerk did not want to lose the big bag of money. "Of course, young man," he said. He gave the boy his money, counting it out, peso by peso.

"That young man is my customer," he said to the father. "If a boy like that can trust me, so can you."

"That's good," said the father. "I wanted to be sure this was the place my son left his money. Now I don't think you'll be interested in what I have." And he rolled the buttons and old metal washers onto the counter.

Then the father put his hand on his son's shoulder and said, "Always be careful of baldheads, son!"

They left the shop and went home. ▲

UNDERSTANDING WHAT YOU READ

Answer the questions below.

1. Why did the boy leave the money at the House of Safekeeping?
2. Why did the clerk return the bag?

VOCABULARY

A. *Read the sentences. Circle the letter of the correct meaning for the underlined words. Use the meanings from the story.*

1. The son went <u>merrily</u> into the town.
   a. sadly
   b. happily
   c. slowly

2. He <u>wandered</u> along for a while.
   a. ran
   b. moved without a special direction
   c. hurried

3. It's <u>foolish</u> for me to carry all this money.
   a. unwise
   b. easy
   c. difficult

4. <u>Have no fear</u>. All your money is quite safe here.
   a. Be afraid.
   b. I'm afraid.
   c. Don't worry.

5. The money I left <u>a little while ago</u>.
   a. an hour or so before
   b. last year
   c. tomorrow

6. Stop <u>wasting</u> my time.
   a. wearing
   b. using up
   c. selling

7. The young man went home feeling very <u>depressed</u>.

    a. cheerful

    b. unhappy

    c. friendly

B. *Write your own sentences using the words below.*

merrily   _____

_____

wander   _____

_____

foolish   _____

_____

waste   _____

_____

depressed   _____

_____

DISCUSSION

1. Why do you think the father said, "Beware of baldheads"?
2. How would you describe the clerk?
3. How would you describe the boy's father?

TELL IT YOUR WAY

Do you know any other stories in which someone tries to trick a young person? If so, tell the story to the class. If not, make up a story with your group or class.

CHARGE IT TO THE CAP

BEFORE YOU READ

Answer the following questions.

1. What does the title mean?
2. How do you charge things at a store or business?
3. What do you see in the illustration?

USING WHAT YOU KNOW

Find the meaning for each word. Then write the letters of the correct meanings on the lines.

_d_	1. cap	a.	man
_____	2. fellow	b.	round white things that come from an oyster
_____	3. rude	c.	move the head up and down to say yes
_____	4. revenge	d.	small hat
_____	5. nod	e.	not polite
_____	6. pearls	f.	hurting someone who has hurt you

nce there was a man named John the Poor. He was so poor that he could hardly feed his family. John the Poor lived next door to a rich fellow named Paul Moneybags.

John the Poor kept getting poorer and poorer. One day he said to his wife, "My dear, I am going next door to ask our rich neighbor for help. I'm sure he won't let us starve." So he dressed carefully and went next door.

Paul Moneybags laughed unkindly. "What a sight you are!" he said. "Just look at you! You're wearing nothing but rags. Your shirt is torn, your trousers have holes in them, and look at your cap!" The rich man doubled over with laughter.

John looked at his hat. It was very old, and it had many holes in it. Still it was a lot better than nothing.

Paul Moneybags stopped laughing long enough to say, "That cap will fall apart at any moment. There are too many holes for the fingers of both hands."

John the Poor put his hat on his head and left. He could hear his rude neighbor laughing behind him.

John took his family and moved away to live in another place.

Three years passed. John made some money. John returned to the district. He had a plan to get revenge on Paul Moneybags for being so unkind.

John bought himself a new cap. It was gray, with a bright blue ribbon. He wore the cap to visit the watchmaker's shop.

"My friend," he said. "I need your help. Over the years Paul Moneybags has been rude and unkind to me. I want to get my revenge. Will you help me? Do you have a cheap watch?"

"Yes, indeed," the watchmaker replied.

"Let me buy it," John said. So he bought the watch and said to the watchmaker, "I want to leave the watch here. Please change the price on it so it seems to be very expensive."

The watchmaker nodded. "I can do that," he said. "Why do you want the watch to have a new price tag?"

"It's part of my plan," John said. "When I come back, I want you to pretend you have never seen me. I shall choose the watch. Then I will say, 'Charge it to the cap!' and you will look at my cap and say, 'Of course, sir. You owe me nothing.'"

The watchmaker agreed.

Then John went to see the owner of the jewelry store. "Can you show me your cheapest pearls?" he asked.

"Here they are," the jeweler replied. "They're artificial, but they look quite real. And they're not at all expensive. I can let you have them for fifty dollars."

John paid for the pearls, and then asked the jeweler to change the price tag. He left the pearls at the shop. "When I come back," he said to the jeweler, "I will ask you for the pearls. When you ask for payment, I will say 'Charge it to the cap.' You will look straight at my cap and say 'Of course, sir. You owe me nothing.'"

John then went to another shop and bought a suit of clothes. He made the same arrangement as before. The shopkeeper agreed to look at the gray cap and say, "Of course, sir, you owe me nothing."

John visited the inn. Then he set off for the home of Paul Moneybags.

Paul saw that John looked well dressed, so he greeted him courteously. "Come in, my friend," he said. "You look very elegant. That's a very fine cap you're wearing."

"It's useful to me," John said. "But really! I'm not here to talk about my cap! I've come to ask you to go to town with me. I have to do a little shopping. Then I would like you to have a meal with me. I'll pay, of course."

"Thank you," Paul Moneybags said. "I will be honored to be your guest." And he thought to himself, "Good! Now, I'll get a meal for nothing."

John and Paul went first to the watchmaker's shop. "I want you to show me your best watch," John said.

The watchmaker pulled out the watch John had bought earlier in the day. "This is my most expensive watch," he said.

"Money isn't a problem," John said. "I like it, so I'll take it. Just charge it to the cap."

The watchmaker looked at John's gray cap and said, "Of course, sir. You owe me nothing."

Paul Moneybags could hardly believe his ears.

John led Paul to the jeweler's. "I need to see your most expensive pearls for my wife," he said.

The jeweler took out the artificial pearls. The new price tag read five hundred dollars.

"I'll take them," John said grandly. "Just charge them to the cap!"

"Of course, sir," the jeweler replied. He looked at John's cap and bowed. "You owe me nothing."

Paul Moneybags was speechless. They went to the next shop. Paul watched in silence as John picked out a new suit and charged it to the cap.

At last it was time to go to the inn for lunch. They had a large meal, and John said to the innkeeper, "Charge it to the cap." The innkeeper bowed and said,

"Certainly, sir. You owe me nothing."

John and Paul left the inn.

"Will you sell me your cap?" Paul asked.

"I love my cap," John replied.

"Please, I must have it," Paul begged. "Please, I want it badly. I'll give you twenty thousand dollars for it."

"I can't give up my beautiful cap," John said. He sounded a little doubtful.

Paul begged some more. Then at last he said, "I'll give you forty thousand dollars. That's a lot for a cap."

"All right," John replied. "I'll let you have it. I know how much you want it." And he sold Paul the cap and said goodbye.

Paul Moneybags rushed home. "Quickly, my dear!" he called to his wife. "Come shopping with me. I'll buy you anything you want."

"Anything?" his wife asked. "Even diamonds and gold?"

"Anything," Paul replied.

So Paul put on the cap and they hurried into town. They went to the very best jewelry store. Paul Moneybags' wife put a diamond necklace around her neck and smiled at him.

"You shall have it, my dear," Paul said. He turned to the jeweler. "Charge it to the cap," he said.

"What did you say?" the jeweler asked.

Paul touched his gray cap. "Charge it to the cap," he repeated. "I don't have to pay for this necklace."

Paul and his wife walked out the door but they didn't get very far. The jeweler came out and called, "Stop, thief!" Soon, the police came and took Paul Moneybags away.

Now John the Poor is John the Rich. He lives in luxury.

Poor Paul Moneybags is quite crazy and is living in a mental asylum. He talks to anyone who comes near him. He shows them a gray cap and says, "You can buy things with this cap! I know, I've seen it work!"

Of course, nobody believes him. ▲

UNDERSTANDING WHAT YOU READ

A. *Answer the questions below.*

1. How did Paul Moneybags treat John the Poor?
2. How did John the Poor trick Paul Moneybags?

B. *Circle the word that best completes each sentence.*

John the Poor asked Paul Moneybags for (help, gold, animals). Paul (laughed, smiled, yelled) at him very rudely. John went away. When he came back, he had a (pearl, plan, watch) to trick Paul. John went around town and bought (cheap, gray, old) things. Then, the shopkeepers changed the prices so they looked (ragged, clever, expensive). John took Paul to the shops. Paul thought John could (buy, use, leave) things by saying, "Charge it to the cap."

VOCABULARY

A. *Read the sentences. Circle the letter of the correct meaning for the underlined words. Use the meanings from the story.*

1. My dear, I am going next door to ask our rich <u>neighbor</u> for help.
   a. someone who lends money
   b. someone who lives nearby
   c. someone who is poor

2. I'm sure he won't let us <u>starve</u>.
   a. die of hunger
   b. leave your home
   c. give things away

3. You're wearing nothing but <u>rags</u>. Your shirt is torn, your trousers have holes in them.
   a. holes
   b. old, torn clothes
   c. no clothes

4. John returned to the <u>district</u>.

    a. area

    b. school

    c. hospital

5. They're <u>artificial</u>, but they look quite real.

    a. pretty

    b. made by man, not natural

    c. useful

6. He made the same <u>arrangement</u> as before.

    a. plan

    b. joke

    c. mistake

7. Paul saw that John looked well dressed, so he greeted him <u>courteously</u>.

    a. rudely

    b. politely

    c. stupidly

8. Paul Moneybags was <u>speechless</u>. Paul watched in silence.

    a. happy

    b. miserable

    c. unable to speak

9. "Please, I must have it," Paul <u>begged</u>. "Please, I want it so much."

    a. began

    b. asked over and over

    c. ordered

10. Poor Paul Moneybags is quite <u>crazy</u> and is living in a mental asylum.

    a. lazy

    b. hungry

    c. mad

B. Go back to the story and find words and phrases that tell us what Paul Moneybags and John the Poor were like. Write them below. Three have been done for you.

Paul Moneybags   John the Poor

rich   *poor*

laughed unkindly

DISCUSSION

1. Do you feel sorry for Paul Moneybags? Why? Why not?
2. Pretend you are Ms. Moneybags. Tell the story to a friend.

TELL IT YOUR WAY

A. Look back over the story. Find a part of the story that tells how a person in the story felt. Draw a face that shows that feeling. Explain the drawing to the class.

B. Choose your favorite part of the story and illustrate it. Explain your drawing and tell why you like that part of the story.

C. Tell what you think Paul Moneybags and John the Poor (Rich) are like now.

SENAHU AT WAR

BEFORE YOU READ

Answer the following questions.

1. What does the title tell us?
2. What do you need to do before you go to war?
3. What do you see in the illustration?

USING WHAT YOU KNOW

Find the meaning for each word. Then write the letters of the correct meanings on the lines.

_d_	1. message	a.	leader of a group of soldiers
_____	2. telegraph	b.	a group of people ready to fight
_____	3. commandant	c.	a way of sending messages a long distance
_____	4. army	d.	something someone tells you
_____	5. nobly	e.	unable to walk properly
_____	6. lame	f.	defeat someone in a battle
_____	7. conquer	g.	win
_____	8. victory	h.	in a grand, important manner

his is a story about a town in Guatemala called Senahu. It happened at the turn of the century, in the year 1900.

Everything was quiet in Senahu. The people of the town were waking up after a cold night. Most people were still in their houses. A few were starting the day's work.

The town was peaceful and still. No dogs were barking, and the breeze blew gently through the trees. Everything was calm, but all that was going to change.

A message arrived by telegraph. It said, "Jesus Oliva, Local Commandant: Prepare for battle! Prepare immediately! Meet near Panzos." It was signed by the general of the army.

The telegrapher wrote the message on a piece of paper and ran all the way to the commandant's house. Jesus Oliva was just getting up.

"Commandant Jesus Oliva," the telegrapher said, "I have a message for you." He gave a deep bow and handed the piece of paper to Jesus Oliva.

Jesus Oliva looked at the note. He couldn't read it. So he handed the piece of paper back to the telegrapher and said, "Well, what does it say? Speak to me, man. Don't waste time."

The telegrapher cleared his throat and read, "Jesus Oliva, Local Commandant: Prepare for battle! Prepare immediately! Meet near Panzos."

Local Commandant Jesus Oliva stood up very tall. "Then we must fight!" he cried nobly. "Let us sound the alarm! Let us assemble the troops!" And he hurried back into the house.

The telegrapher ran to the church. The priest rang the church bell to tell people to meet in the town square.

Soon the whole town was busy. People hurried like ants from one place to another. The women baked corn bread for the men to take into battle. The men dressed for war. They spoke to each other bravely.

Then somebody said, "Where are our weapons, Jesus Oliva?"

"Weapons?" Jesus Oliva said. "Guns? Swords? I hadn't thought about that."

The people in the square were worried. Then, someone said, "There are guns in the Dieseldorf Warehouse. Let's go there. Let's take those guns so we can defend ourselves."

So everyone went to the warehouse, and each man got a gun. The men came back and loaded their mules. The women said good-bye to them and wept. The children cried loudly.

Jesus Oliva's wife said, "Why don't you take our horse? It can go faster if you have to escape from the enemy."

Jesus Oliva knew his horse was lame. It could only move slowly. "No, my dear!" he said nobly. "We will not need to run away." He took his mule and called the men together. "Let us go fight for our beloved city!" Jesus Oliva cried.

Then the men marched from the town, leaving the women and children behind.

The people of the town gathered in the town square. "Our brave men have gone," a woman said. "Let's leave the town. We can sleep in the woods tonight."

"That's wise," said another woman. "It's better for us in the woods. Then if the enemy attacks, we will be safe."

The people hurried. They gathered their children and their blankets and went to hide in the woods. Just a few brave old people stayed to defend Senahu against the enemy.

Meantime, the men marched to Panzos. They all felt full of courage. They were ready to fight the enemy! They arrived at Panzos, made their camp, and waited to fight. Every man expected to be a great hero.

A day passed, and the enemy did not come. The little army from Senahu waited patiently. Another day passed, and the enemy still did not come. After four boring days, they all marched back to Senahu.

Jesus Oliva went to the post office. He said to the telegrapher, "Send a message to the general of the army. Say: We went to Panzos, but the enemy did not come."

A few hours later a reply came. The telegrapher went to Don Jesus and read aloud, "Commandant, Jesus Oliva: The enemy has been conquered. Celebrate our victory!"

The people gathered to celebrate. They brought out their tambourines, drums, and marimbas. Everyone was ready to enjoy a marvelous party. They gathered at the plaza. Three musicians were playing wonderful music to make people forget all their troubles. The old people sang and remembered the joys of long ago. The young people sang and prepared for the joys of the future.

Don Jesus was enjoying the victory celebration. "I never lost a man!" he told anyone who would listen. "I led all my men home from Panzos."

"The enemy knew we were there!" a man boasted. "They knew how brave we were. That's why they didn't appear. They were too afraid of us."

The telegrapher was busy back at the post office. Another message came down the line. He wrote it down carefully. "Commandant Don Jesus Oliva: Again the enemy will attack! Prepare! Send men!"

The telegrapher hurried to the square and found Don Jesus near the musicians. It was very noisy. The telegrapher handed the commandant the note.

Don Jesus held the note upside down. "What does it say?" he asked. The telegrapher read the message. Just as he spoke there was a loud blast of music. Don Jesus could not hear the telegrapher's reply.

Don Jesus looked wisely at the note and pretended to read it.

He turned to the telegrapher and said, "Send a reply. Say that I am busy dancing."

And that is the end of the story of Senahu at war. As it turned out, there was no war in 1900, so Don Jesus could dance as much as he liked. ▲

UNDERSTANDING WHAT YOU READ

A. *Answer the questions below.*

1. Could Don Jesus read? How did he send and receive messages?
2. Was the town of Senahu ever in danger from the enemy? Why?

B. *Tell if each statement is true, false, or maybe could be true. Write* true, false, *or* maybe *on the lines. Explain your answers to the class.*

false   1. The town was always ready for war.

_____ 2. There was a terrible battle.

_____ 3. Don Jesus was an excellent general.

_____ 4. The telegrapher could read and write.

_____ 5. Don Jesus was very boastful.

_____ 6. The people were wise to hide in the woods.

_____ 7. The people were very excited about going to fight.

_____ 8. Don Jesus' wife was very proud of him.

_____ 9. Everyone had fun at the victory celebration.

VOCABULARY

A. Use the following words to fill in the blanks in the sentences below.

courage   telegrapher   weapon

message   victory   army

lame

1. I want you to give my friend a _____. Please tell her I'll be late.

2. My brother wants to join the _____, but I hope he never has to go to war.

3. A _____ is a person who can use the telegraph to send messages.

4. A gun is a deadly _____.

5. I've hurt my leg. So I'm too _____ to run.

6. I hope you have a great _____ and defeat the enemy.

7. Brave people show great _____.

B. Choose five of the words below. Then use each word in a sentence.

weapon   message   victory

army   lame   courage

telegrapher

_____.

_____.

_____.

_____.

_____.

63

DISCUSSION

1. What advice would you give the commandant?
2. Work with your group or partner to make a description of Don Jesus. Describe his appearance. Tell what kind of person he was.
3. Is life difficult for people who cannot read? Work with your group or class to make a list of the problems of non-readers.

DICTATION

_____

_____

_____

_____

_____

_____

THE MAN WHO SOLD HIS SOUL TO THE DEVIL

BEFORE YOU READ

Answer the following questions.

1. What does the title mean?
2. What do you expect to happen in this story?
3. What do you know about the devil?

USING WHAT YOU KNOW

A. Circle the words that are names for the devil.

Satan	fire	sulfur	Luzbel
ash	Lucifer	handsome	

B. Complete the crossword puzzle.

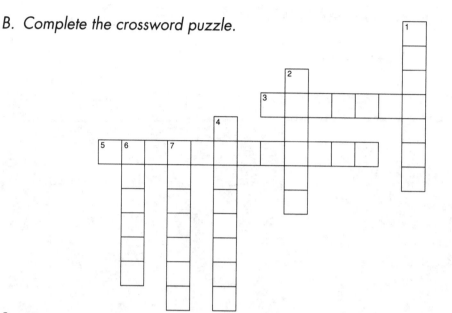

Across

3. a name for the devil
5. with great feeling

Down

1. in a harsh and firm way
2. cleaned by removing dust
4. a legal agreement to do something
6. have enough money to buy or do something
7. said in a mean, nasty way

nce upon a time there was a very poor man named Emeterio Molinari. He lived from day to day. He got poorer and poorer and could not pay his bills.

Emeterio was in love with Rosa, a girl from the village. He longed to marry her, but he knew he could never afford to support a wife.

One day, Emeterio was walking by the river with Rosa. Rosa said, "Emeterio, there is something I must tell you. My father has found someone he wants me to marry. He is not as handsome as you. . ."

Emeterio grabbed her arm and swung her around to face him. "But he is rich, I suppose!" he said. Then he brushed Rosa aside and ran to the broken-down hut where he lived.

"I am so tired of being poor!" he cried. He looked around. His hut was on a rocky, barren piece of land. Nothing grew there. "I wish I had money!" he fell to his knees and said passionately. "I would even take money from the devil himself. I want money! I want money!"

Someone was moving outside. "Who could that be?" Emeterio wondered. "Who do I owe money to?" He crept into a corner and hid.

Emeterio stayed still and watched through a crack in the wall while a stranger knocked on the door. The visitor was a handsome, well dressed man. None of Emeterio's creditors ever looked like that!

The man knocked again. He called, "Emeterio, you called me and I have come. Let me in."

"I didn't call anyone," Emeterio thought. "Still I can let him in. He doesn't look like any of the people I owe money to, and there's nothing for him to steal."

Emeterio opened the door, and the man came in. He carefully dusted a place on Emeterio's dirty old table so he could sit down. Then he said, "Brother, I have come to help you."

"He must be mad," Emeterio thought. "I have no brothers, and nobody helps me." He said aloud, "My brothers are all dead. I think you have made a mistake."

"You called me," the man replied. He was so good looking, he almost glowed. "You invited me here. You even begged me to come — on your knees. You said, 'I would even take money from the devil himself.' Well here I am."

"You mean you're the devil?" Emeterio asked. "You're the devil, himself? You're Lucifer?"

The devil smiled a satisfied smile. "That's right," he said. "I'm the devil. Some people call me Satan; some call me Lucifer or Luzbel. You may call me 'sir.'"

"What are you doing here?" Emeterio asked.

"Not very bright, are you?" the devil sneered. "You called me. You wanted money. I've come to help you." The devil smiled at Emeterio. "I can give you everything you want," he said. "Land, women, money, riches beyond belief. I can let you have them all. I can promise you that Rosa will marry you. Her father will come and beg you to marry her, because you will be the richest man around."

Emeterio thought of all the years of being poor and said, "Nothing is for free. What do you want from me?"

"I want your soul," the devil said. "I have a contract for you. Sign it, and you will have everything you've ever wanted."

Emeterio tried to take the paper. His hand was shaking.

"Steady," the devil said. He put the paper down on the table and spread it out so Emeterio could see it.

Emeterio could hear his own heart beating. The devil touched his hand. Emeterio's skin felt as though a snake was crawling on it.

The devil swiftly pulled out a sharp knife and cut Emeterio's wrist.

He dipped a pen into Emeterio's blood and said, "Sign here! Then you will be able to afford anything you want."

Emeterio felt weak. He signed the contract and immediately fell into a deep sleep. He did not hear the devil laughing as he put the paper where Emeterio would see it when he awakened.

Emeterio woke up late the next morning. He looked around. "Where am I?" he wondered. "I usually sleep on a pile of rags. Now I'm in a soft bed, with clean sheets."

He saw the contract and remembered the day before. He had sold his soul to the devil! "I can't get up," he thought, "because the devil will come and get me." He lay in bed, frozen with fear, waiting for the devil to come back.

There was a knock at the door. "It's him!" Emeterio said. "It's the devil! Why did I do it?" He could hear a man shouting his name, but he was too afraid to listen to the words.

"Emeterio, come out," the man called. "It's Rosa's father. Do you still want to marry my daughter?"

Emeterio put his head under the pillow.

"Emeterio, come out!" Rosa's father called again. "Come and see your farm! It's a miracle!"

Emeterio looked out the window. Yesterday his land had been bare, dry, and brown. Now there were beautiful crops in all the fields.

Yesterday, the only building on his farm was an old hut. Today, he saw clean, freshly painted farm buildings. He was in a room on the second floor of a big house. Roses grew in the garden. Everything was fresh, clean, and beautiful.

"Are you ever going to let me in?" Rosa's father asked.

Emeterio ran down to open the door. Rosa's father stepped onto the room. "My daughter says she will marry no one but you," he said. "I don't know where you got the money, my boy, but you can certainly afford to support a wife. I give my consent. You may marry my Rosa."

Emeterio was too surprised to speak. Rosa's father thought he had changed his mind and didn't want to marry her anymore. "Please, Emeterio," he begged. "Marry my Rosa."

Emeterio thought he could hear the devil laughing. "One one condition," he replied sternly. "I will marry Rosa, but I will not go to a church. The wedding must be here, in this house."

Rosa and Emeterio were married. Poor Rosa worried because she wanted to be blessed by a priest. But Emeterio would not hear of it. He loved Rosa, so whenever she got upset he bought her something — a diamond necklace, a gold bracelet, or some other piece of jewelry.

Years passed. Rosa had a son, and then another, and then another. Emeterio grew richer and richer.

Emeterio's sons were growing into fine men. He loved them all, but the eldest boy, Candelario, was the apple of his eye. Every evening, father and son would take a walk around the garden and talk together. It was the best part of the day for Emeterio.

One day, Candelario said, "I have something serious to ask you, father. I am so fortunate to be your son. You have given me everything. But there is just one thing that I want."

"What is that, my son?" Emeterio asked. "Whatever you want you will have."

"I want to be a priest," Candelario replied.

"Get out of my sight!" Emeterio cried. "Go! And never suggest such a thing again!" He tore a stick from a tree and beat Candelario all the way to the house.

As soon as Candelario was inside, Emeterio went to his room and called the devil. There was a puff of smoke and a nasty smell of burning, and the devil appeared.

"What shall I do?" Emeterio asked.

"You will not let the boy be a priest. Do you understand?" the devil answered. And before Emeterio could reply, the devil disappeared.

Nothing was ever the same again. Emeterio became depressed and stayed alone in his room. He went to sleep, but he had bad dreams. Worst of all, Candelario avoided him. There were no more evening walks in the garden.

At last, Emeterio decided to look at the contract he had signed so long ago. He read it carefully and found a clause he had never seen before. His contract would run out in two years.

Emeterio didn't really care. He was sad all the time, and nothing could make him happy. It was as though he were living in a dark cloud, and every day the cloud grew thicker and darker. He continued to grow richer and richer, but his money didn't make him happy.

The two years passed. Emeterio went out gambling. In one night, he lost the farm. He was very surprised to find that he didn't care. "Perhaps I can't feel anything anymore," he thought.

When he got home, Rosa greeted him in tears. "It's Candelario," she wept. "He's hot and cold — one minute burning with fever, the next as cold as ice."

Emeterio found he still had feelings; Rosa's news made him feel the most terrible pain and grief. He hurried to see his son, but the boy did not know who he was. Emeterio looked at him for a long time and wept.

Then Emeterio kissed Rosa goodbye and went into the woods to sit under a tree and wait.

The devil appeared almost immediately. "Nice tree," he said. "Good, strong branches. It's a fine hanging tree." He threw a rope over the highest branch.

"Can't I have a little longer?" Emeterio asked.

The devil laughed at him. "I have your soul," he said. "You're mine. I gave you everything I promised."

"And you took it away," Emeterio said.

"Well, that's my right," the devil said. "Now, hurry and hang yourself. I'd have taken you weeks ago, but your wife and children kept praying for you. See? I brought you a rope. I'm looking after you right up to the end."

Emeterio did what he was told. He took the rope and hanged himself. The people of the little town found him a few days later. His whole body was black, and the tree was covered with a black ash. A horrible smell of sulphur hung over the place.

The people spoke in quiet voices. "I swear," an old man said. "This is evil. I tell you, it is the work of the devil."

Nobody disagreed. ▲

UNDERSTANDING WHAT YOU READ

Answer the following questions.

1. Why did Emeterio sell his soul?
2. Was he happy when he first got rich?
3. Was he happy at the end of the story?

VOCABULARY

Read the sentences. Circle the letter of the correct meaning for the underlined words. Use the meanings from the story.

1. He <u>longed</u> to marry her.

   a. wanted

   b. had

   c. couldn't

2. Land, women, money, riches <u>beyond belief</u>.

   a. as usual

   b. in unbelievable amounts

   c. like everyone else

3. Candelario was the <u>apple of his eye</u>.

   a. his favorite

   b. his garden

   c. his wife

4. "<u>Get out of my sight!</u>" Emeterio cried.

   a. Let me see you!

   b. Come here!

   c. Go away!

5. Can't I have <u>a little longer</u>?

   a. more time

   b. more distance

   c. some money

DISCUSSION

1. How do you feel about Emeterio? Was he an evil man? Why? Why not?
2. Would you sell your soul to the devil?
3. What do you think happened to Candelario?
4. What would have happened if Rosa had refused to marry Emeterio outside a church?

TELL IT YOUR WAY

A. *Do you know any stories about the devil? If so, tell the story to the class. If not, make up a story with your group or class.*

B. *Make another ending to the story.*

SUGGESTED READING FOR THE TEACHER

or theoretical underpinning, you may like to read these references. They are drawn from the two disciplines of teaching reading to ESL students and teaching reading to remedial students.

Cameron, Penelope. Some Considerations When Writing a Guided Reader. ERIC ED 295 469, 1988.

Carrell, Patricia L. "A View of Written Text as Communicative Interaction." In Research in Reading in English as a Second Language, edited by Devine, Carrell, and Eskey, TESOL, 1987.

Carrell, Patricia L. "Content and Formal Schemata in ESL Reading." TESOL Quarterly Volume 21, Number 3, 1987.

Eskey, David E. "Comments on Devine." In Research in Reading in English as a Second Language, edited by Devine, Carrell, and Eskey, TESOL, 1987.

Greenwood, Jean. Class Readers. Oxford University Press, 1988.

McCormick, Sandra. Remedial and Clinical Reading Instruction. Merrill, 1987.

Rhodes and Dudley-Marling. Readers and Writers with a Difference: a Holistic Approach to Teaching Learning Disabled and Remedial Students. Heinemann Educational Books, 1988.

Spencer and Sadoski. "Differential Effects Among Cultural Groups of Prereading Activities in ESL." Reading Psychology: An International Quarterly. 9:227-232, 1988.

Steffensen, Margaret S. "The Effect of Context and Culture on Children's L2 Reading: A Review." In Research in Reading in English as a Second Language, edited by Devine, Carrell, and Eskey, TESOL, 1987.

Taglieber, Johnson, and Yarbrough. "Effects of Prereading Activities on ESL Reading by Brazilian College Students." TESOL Quarterly Volume 22, Number 3, 1988.

Wilson and Cleland. Diagnostic and Remedial Reading for Classroom and Clinic, 6th Edition. Merrill, 1989.

SUGGESTIONS AND ANSWER KEY FOR THE TEACHER

PEDRO DE URDEMALAS AND THE PIGS' TAILS

Suggestions

The pre-reading exercises should be done cooperatively, as a class, in small groups, or in pairs. Be sure the students recognize the pigs' tails in the illustration.

Answers

Using What You Know

1. d   2. a   3. e   4. b   5. f   6. c

Understanding What You Read

A.   1. true   2. true   3. false   4. false   5. true
     6. false   7. false
B.   bad, cut off, swamp, kind, pigs, ran away

Vocabulary

A.   1. ranch   2. liar   3. swamp   4. weep

LA LLORONA

Suggestions

Have the students mime sad, weeping, sleepy, and terrified and then put them into sentences.

Read the dictation passage to the students at normal conversational speed. Then read it again, pausing frequently for them to write. Then read it again at normal speed.

Answers

Using What You Know

sob, crying, weeping, cry, wailing

Understanding What You Read

1. She was looking for her children.
2. He saw La Llorona and died of fright.

Vocabulary

A.   1. a   2. c   3. c   4. a   5. a

Dictation

La Llorona was a cruel woman. She drowned her babies. Then, she walked through the streets. She was looking for her babies. She cried and sobbed. All the people of Mexico City were afraid. At last, La Llorona went away.

THE HIDDEN GOLD MINE

Suggestions

The conversations between Quintana and the priest — before and after the priest goes to the mine — can be used as a role play.

Answers
Using What You Know
1. b   2. d   3. e   4. c   5. a

Understanding What You Read
1. 5   2. 3   3. 6   4. 1   5. 2   6. 4

Vocabulary
1. b   2. a   3. b   4. c   5. c   6. a

PEDRO DE URDEMALAS AND THE MAGIC COOKING POT

Suggestions

The students know about Pedro because they have read the first story, "Pedro de Urdemalas and the Pigs' Tails." Remind them of the story before they do the exercise "Using What You Know."

Read the dictation passage to the students at normal conversational speed. Then read it again, pausing frequently for them to write. Then read it again at normal speed.

Answers
Using What You Know
clever, trickster, liar

Understanding What You Read
1. 1   2. 6   3. 3   4. 5   5. 2   6. 4

Vocabulary
1. c   2. a   3. b   4. c   5. a   6. b   7. b

Dictation

Pedro was clever. He made a fire. Then he put the fire into a hole. He set his pot on it. He said the pot boiled water without a fire. A stranger bought the pot. Pedro told him to wait quietly. Pedro ran away.

THE BOBO RIDES ON A BROOM

Suggestions

Be sure to point out that there are no witches in the illustration.

When a student is telling the story using the voice of the Bobo, his partner can pretend not to believe him. Allow students to make notes before they speak.

The group discussion exercise can be done in small groups, with one member of the group reporting to the class.

Answers

Using What You Know

1. c   2. f   3. b   4. e   5. d   6. a

Understanding What You Read

A. 1. A bobo is a stupid person who gets everything wrong.
    2. He fell because he forgot the spell
    3. They ran away because they thought he was the devil.
    4. He heard stories about witches. Sometimes they turn people into birds, animals, or even snakes.

B. 1. 2   2. 5   3. 3   4. 6   5. 1   6. 7   7. 4

Vocabulary

1. gather
2. chattered
3. scary
4. flooding
5. was very curious
6. made up his mind
7. soared
8. no good
9. flapped
10. landed

PEDRO DE URDEMALAS SELLS A TREE

Suggestions

Remind the students about the other stories about Pedro.

The grid is subjective. There are no right or wrong answers.

When the students draw the story, a few can put it on the board, while others make suggestions. This exercise teaches segmenting a story.

When the students mime, check to see that their body language is appropriate.

Answers

Using What You Know

amazed, fierce, hold, nice, scared

Understanding What You Read

1. e   2. c   3. b   4. f   5. a   6. d

Vocabulary

1. exhausted
2. amazed
3. pick
4. fierce
5. bears
6. protect it
7. take me for a fool
8. a nasty way
9. Have it your way.
10. It's a deal.

FOOL'S DAY

Suggestions

Have the students mime the way a proud person looks, moves, and walks.

If the students cannot explain what Don Ramiro would do at the end of the story, let them mime it.

If there are students from the same culture in the class, have them compare descriptions of Fool's Day in their country. Then have them report back to the larger group. This can be done as an oral or a written exercise.

Answers

Using What You Know

1. c   2. g   3. b   4. e   5. d   6. a   7. f

Understanding What You Read

proud, family, trick, angry, letter, Poor fool

Vocabulary

proud, boastful, foolish, not a bad man, respectable, honest, gave to charity, kind to the poor

THE SHARK HUNTER

Suggestions

Be sure that students know what sharks are and how frightening they can be.

The shark vocabulary can be used to create a semantic map. Write the word *shark* in a circle at the center of the blackboard. Ask the students for the words that they associate with sharks. Write the words on the board, clustering related ideas.

If the students mime the "feelings" exercises, choose the best student to mime for the class, but don't tell the class which emotion is being mimed. Make them figure it out.

Answers

Understanding What You Read

A. 1. Rufino was afraid because he lost the medallion. He thought the Virgin Carmen would not protect him.

    2. He hoped the Virgin Carmen would protect him even without the medallion. He wanted to marry Maria.

B. 1. 2   2. 6   3. 5   4. 1   5. 3   6. 4

C. 1. false   2. false   3. true   4. true   5. true

Using What You Know

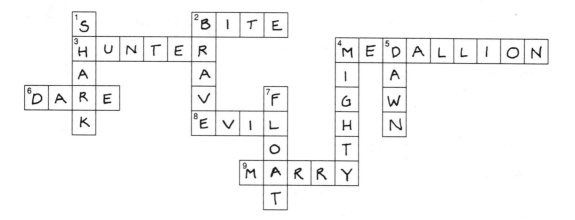

JUAN DIEGO AND THE VIRGIN OF GUADALUPE

Suggestions

Be sure the students understand the words *angel*, *bishop*, *church*, *priest*, *last rites*, and *cape*.

Let a student recount this story orally. If the student cannot define or describe Juan Diego's feelings, let him or her mime them.

Because this is a well-loved story, ask the students to choose a favorite passage to read aloud.

If it is suitable for your students, have them write a script for the role play.

Answers

Understanding What You Read

1. The Virgin wanted the church built on Tepeyac Hill.
2. The bishop didn't believe Juan Diego's story.
3. Yes.

BEWARE OF BALDHEADS

Suggestions

Be sure that the students know the meanings of the words in the exercise "Using What You Know."

Elicit the information that a bag of buttons and metal washers can be mistaken for coins.

Answers

Using What You Know

washers, ago, merrily, while, clerk, money, on, **one**

Understanding What You Read

1. He wanted to keep it safe. He trusted the clerk to return it.
2. He wanted to get the big bag from the father.

Vocabulary

A. 1. b   2. b   3. a   4. c   5. a   6. b   7. b

CHARGE IT TO THE CAP

Suggestions

Be sure that students understand the idea of charging something: Most people know about credit cards.

Try to elicit explanations and illustrations of revenge, or have the students act out the idea of revenge.

In the exercise in which students write characteristics of Paul Moneybags and John the Poor, permit wide interpretation.

Answers

Using What You Know

1. d   2. a   3. e   4. f   5. c   6. b

Understanding What You Read

A. 1. Paul Moneybags was rude and unkind to John the Poor.

 2. John the Poor made Paul Moneybags believe he could buy things with his cap.

B. help, laughed, plan, cheap, expensive, buy

Vocabulary

A. 1. b 2. a 3. b 4. a 5. b

 6. a 7. b 8. c 9. b 10. c

SENAHU AT WAR

Suggestions

The advice to the commandant can take the form of a role play — commandant/wife or commandant/soldier.

The list of problems of illiterate people can be a blackboard group learning activity.

Read the dictation passage to the students at normal conversational speed. Then read it again, pausing frequently for them to write. Then read it again at normal conversational speed.

Answers

Using What You Know

1. d 2. c 3. a 4. b 5. h 6. e 7. f 8. g

Understanding What You Read

A. 1. No. He sent and received messages by telegraph.

 2. No. There was no war in 1900.

B. 1. false   4. true   7. true/maybe

 2. false   5. true   8. maybe

 3. false   6. maybe   9. maybe

Vocabulary

A. 1. message 2. army 3. telegrapher 4. weapon

 5. lame 6. victory 7. courage

Dictation

Don Jesus was the commandant of the army. He did not know how to read. He did not even think about guns for his army. Somebody else told him where to find them. However, his people were brave. They were ready to fight for their town. It was very lucky that there really was no war.

THE MAN WHO SOLD HIS SOUL TO THE DEVIL

Suggestions

Use vocabulary about the devil to create a semantic map. Put the word devil in a circle in the center of the blackboard. Ask the students for words they associate with the devil. Write the words on the blackboard, clustering related ideas. Include the names Satan, Lucifer, and Luzbel and the words *fire*, *ash*, and *sulfur*.

Answers

Using What You Know

A. Satan, Luzbel, Lucifer

B.

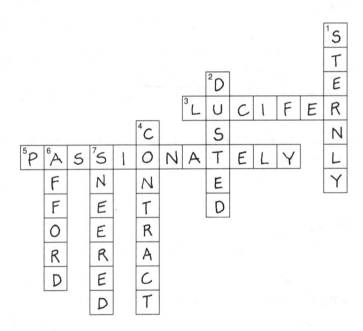

Understanding What You Read

1. He wanted money. He was tired of being poor.
2. Yes.
3. No.

Vocabulary

1. a   2. b   3. a   4. c   5. a